HIDDEN POND

HIDDEN POND

By HELEN GIRVAN

ILLUSTRATED BY ALBERT ORBAAN

For Marjorie

Table of Contents

HIDDEN POND

CHAPTER I

The Wrong Train

WHEN IT BEGAN to drizzle Denis hugged her coat closer with a shiver of misgiving. Although the watch her mother had given her when she was graduated from high school in June was on her wrist, once more she walked back and looked at the waiting room clock. Ten minutes after six. That meant another twenty minutes before her local train was due.

An hour had not seemed long to wait when she was put off the Montreal express at this isolated junction in French Canada. The station, with its tidy beds of petunias, was foreign enough to be interesting, and its name, Côte L'Avenir, invited speculation.

But Denis had soon seen all there was to see. There were no other passengers and she could understand but little of the station agent's French; the waiting room was stuffy and there were no benches outside. As she walked up and down the deserted platform, the approaching dusk made the poor aspect of the surrounding country even more depressing.

All that September day heavy clouds, like a thick, tufted grey quilt, had pressed ominously low over the fields and woods. When the clouds broke in a steady drizzle, Denis shivered and gave the station sign a wry glance as she walked back to look at the clock. The Future indeed! If L'Avenir was a taste of what she might expect at *Manoir Laurent* with her father's brother and his family, the immediate future looked pretty dim.

Uncle Guy himself was a lamb. When he stopped off in Ohio to see them last month, Denis had liked him at once. He had arrived, it so happened, shortly after her mother received the letter from Texas. Since Mrs. Fraser made her living as an interior decorator, the opportunity to do a large ranch house there could not be dismissed lightly. But she was loath to be away for what would probably be most of the winter, especially now that the doctor had insisted Denis must not enter music school as planned for at least a year. Nor must she take a job, unless it was walking someone's dog. Because she must be in the open air as much as possible.

"Why not send Denis up to *Manoir Laurent* for the winter?" said Uncle Guy. "It's rugged but healthy. And she ought to know her father's old home."

Mrs. Fraser had snatched at the solution and Denis had been eager to come, partly because she did not know what else to do. At *Manoir Laurent*, of course, she could be out-of-doors as prescribed and it would be an adventure even if it was a lost year.

Moreover, Denis was anxious to see her father's old home and that of the famous grandfather for whom she was named. But no one had prepared her for the bleakness of the countryside, so flat and dull and lonely. She remembered that her grandfather, with whom she had fallen in love at their one brief meeting, would not be at *Manoir Laurent*. She liked Uncle Guy but Aunt Felice was a stranger. Perhaps the Frenchwoman might not welcome an addition to her family. And suppose the three—or was it four—cousins did not speak English?

As the drizzle became real rain, her misgivings increased. On a day all too like this in June something had happened to her. It was a Sunday, the day she was to play at her first recital and from the time she was seven Denis had spent five hours each day at the piano in preparation for that event. This daily practice left little enough time for lessons much less play. She could not join in the games or sports, or go to dances as the other girls and boys in high school did. And on the rare occasions when Denis forgot she was to be a concert pianist, Mrs. Fraser reminded her of the fact.

Once, for a school concert, she had wanted to accompany the soloist but her mother would not hear of it.

"But why, mother? Mary Sargent has such a good voice."

"If she were Marian Anderson it would make no difference. You are not going to accompany *anyone*. You are to be a concert pianist."

But in spite of the fact that she was to play at her first recital that Sunday afternoon, Denis had been permitted to go to the last class dance the Friday before. She had even had a new dress for the occasion, a yellow dance frock that matched the gold lights in her brown hair. And when Sid Ford, the most popular boy in the class, with whom Denis had never discussed anything but the horrors of mathematics, asked for a dance, she had smiled astonished pleasure.

"Whew, Brown Eyes! You ought to smile oftener," Sid told her.

After that she had danced and danced and made three dates for the next day none of which she was allowed to keep. But in spite of a Saturday of complete rest, Denis awoke the morning of the recital feeling as dull and heavy as the day. By the time she sat down at the piano to go over the selections she would play later, the chill drizzle had become a driving rain and her fingers were cold. She lifted her hands, then dropped them and stared blankly at the instrument. Something had happened to her. She did not know what to do with her stiff fingers and could not remember a note.

After that everything was hazy. Dr. Lovel came; and the ceiling above Denis's bed became her world. The widest crack was the Mississippi, but day after day she fell asleep before she could count the tributaries. By early August she was downstairs again but the doctor said there must be no serious piano practice for at least a year.

"No practice, mind. You can play to amuse yourself if you like."

Denis knew she would not do that. She had never been permitted to play popular music and now she hated the sight of a piano, anyway. But her mother looked so disturbed that she had felt obliged to demur.

"Then it will be a wasted winter."

"Health is never a waste," snorted Dr. Lovel. "And what's

a year at seventeen? Remember, it's not how fast but how well you travel that counts."

Then Uncle Guy had arrived and apparently solved their problems. Or had he, after all? Perhaps she should have become a Dog Walker and boarded with the people who rented the upstairs part of their house.

In her preoccupation Denis had walked beyond the covered portion of the platform out into the rain. With a quick shake she turned back just in time to see a car drive up and deposit a man and a boy. The former had the self-important air of many short men but the boy, who was about her own age or possibly a little younger, was different.

He was a thin boy, slightly taller than his father but still not tall. He wore a brownish tweed suit, a jaunty yellow tie and he was tanned a healthy brown. Yet he looked pale. It was his curiously haunted look that gave the impression, Denis concluded, as she passed them and overheard a remark that told her the two were waiting for the express to Montreal.

When she approached them on her next round, the boy was speaking earnestly and Denis was struck again by his almost desperate expression. When the older man only shrugged aside his plea as not worth considering, the boy's hopeless look of disappointment was enough to arouse anyone's sympathy. Moreover, Denis could remember a time when she had felt just like that herself.

It was soon after her father's death so she must have been about eight years old. A neighbor had given her a puppy and Denis had begged to keep it. But her mother said a dog would be too much trouble and anyway they could not afford one. A few days later she had found the kitten, a grubby, half-starved mite of black fur, and knew she must have it. She had slipped in the back way, wiped off its paws, three of which proved to be white like tiny boots, and fed the kitten some milk so that it was snuggled into her neck purring content when she sought her mother.

Unfortunately there was a visitor in the living room talking to Mrs. Fraser, a man with silvery grey hair and very black eyes, a handsome man. He was her grandfather, it seemed, and Denis was told to put the kitten out at once, that he wanted her to play the piano for him. When she merely clung unhappily to her treasure and did not move, the man smiled understanding.

"I'll hold the little cat while you play," he offered. And in his laughing black eyes Denis read a willingness to conspire.

She went reluctantly to the piano then and played the piece her mother selected. Since it happened to be the one she had practiced most, she played without a mistake. But her mind was on the kitten; she got through the piece as quickly as possible.

Her grandfather, a world-famous pianist, Denis learned after his departure, thanked her politely without further comment. Instead, he spent the remainder of his short visit persuading her mother to let Denis keep the kitten. And thereby won her heart.

Did the thin boy want something as desperately as she had wanted that kitten? When she passed the two again he was staring straight ahead hopelessly and it was the older man who was talking. Denis caught a scrap of what he said, in a brusk, don't-argue-with-me tone.

"——out of the question. I'll listen to no more of that sort of nonsense, Jarret."

The name Jarret suited the boy somehow, Denis was thinking, when the muffled wail of a train whistle sent her hurrying back to the waiting room for her suitcase. The train proved to be the Montreal Express, however, and Denis watched the boy and his father board it, with the feeling that an absorbing story was being taken from her before she could read the outcome.

When her own train pulled in, their express was still taking water. From a window seat in her local, Denis could look across the platform and see the man and the boy in the other train. Or rather she saw the man, his face pressed against the window as he peered out. Then just before her own train

began to move she was startled to see the boy. Something must have been forgotten for he was on the platform, running toward the waiting room.

The local jerked, moved, gathered speed; rain streamed down the car windows and Côte L'Avenir was left behind. But the boy's frustrated face remained with Denis and would, she knew, for a long time. Automatically, when she heard the car door open, she reached for her purse, found her ticket and looked up expecting to see the conductor. Instead, she looked straight into the harried grey eyes of the boy Jarret, about to take the seat just ahead of hers.

"But you're on the wrong train," Denis protested in consternation.

The boy gave a start of recognition, hesitated and then moved forward and took the seat beside her.

"But this is the local," she repeated in distress.

Jarret's mouth tightened. "I know," he said.

Denis flushed and turned, chin high, to gaze unseeing from the window. If he meant to imply that it was no concern of hers whether he was on the express, the local or—or a camel, he was quite right. It was of neither concern nor interest, she decided proudly and continued to gaze resolutely out the rain-spattered window, unaware that Jarret was inspecting her.

The eyes that had looked up at him in anxious protest were brown, the soft brown of a beaver's fur. Now he saw that the light brown hair had gold lights and that the small, slightly upturned nose belied its owner's arrogant chin and the indifferent set of her mouth. In spite of the lovely hair, she had an indoor, hothouse look that Jarret did not fancy, but something—the high cheek bones perhaps—gave her a certain distinction and she could be trusted, he decided at length.

"I'm—running away," he confided abruptly.

As Denis faced him in astonished concern, the car door opened once more and the conductor came in.

"Are you going to tell?" Jarret challenged in an undertone.

Denis shot him a look of disdain before she again took out her ticket, handed it to the conductor and turned contemptuously to the window. But she could not help hearing her companion buy a ticket to Trois Lacs. Why, that was the station just beyond her own, she remembered from the timetable.

The conductor passed on but Jarret was silent and Denis continued to gaze obstinately out the window while she struggled against the urge to question him. The train jerked to a stop at the next station and after a false start bumped on again before he spoke.

"Thanks for not giving me away. I haven't robbed a bank, you know. It was just that I—couldn't stick college. Not without trying——" He broke off, shrugged and left it at that.

Denis did not know what to say. Her companion had unbuttoned his tweed jacket and as she hesitated, at a loss, his yellow tie drew her attention. On it was a spot or stain so exactly the shape of a beetle that a nervous giggle all but escaped her. "Your—father?" she stammered finally. "Will he know where you are?"

"I hope not," Jarret said emphatically.

"Won't he be—worried?" said Denis, remembering the older man's face as he peered out the train window.

"I'll manage to let him know I'm all right. Everything will be fine unless"—Jarret faced her in instant suspicion—"unless you are questioned and say where I got off."

"I won't see you get off," Denis informed him with dignity. "My station is Laurentville."

"Oh!" Jarret surveyed her with a startled interest he failed to conceal, but after a moment only asked casually, "Laurentville your home?"

"No, I am just going to spend the winter with my uncle who has a farm there. The place is called *Manoir Laurent*. Do you know it?"

Jarret did not respond at once. When he did, it was to evade an answer by saying, "There is such a place near Laurentville."

"What is it like?" Denis persisted. "Flat and dull like Côte L'Avenir?"

Her companion shook his head. "Laurentville is in rolling country and the mountains are only a few miles away. Plenty of lakes around there. Great fishing! Wonderful ski country!" His eyes shone, the words spilled out in resonant tones; he was suddenly animated, glowing with enthusiasm.

"And *Manoir Laurent?*" Denis prompted, convinced that he knew the place.

"Oh, not bad." He shrugged, the haunted look returned and suddenly Jarret gathered up his package, grabbed his hat and muttered something about a smoke as he stood up.

"Well, have a good winter, eh? And thanks again."

He had started down the aisle before Denis could respond, leaving her with her mouth half open. Exasperated, she watched him pass into the car ahead. Now she could not find out what he knew about *Manoir Laurent* and never would know why he was running away. Because what could possibly be so bad about college as to make anyone want to run away before he got there?

The train had slowed up for a station now and when it

finally stopped Denis moved to a seat across the aisle and looked out in the hope of seeing where they were. This was La Baie, she discovered, and remained to watch the few passengers who left the train. One hurried into a waiting car, another climbed into a horse-driven vehicle and a third opened his umbrella and vanished into the darkness and rain. There was still a fourth, Denis noticed. With his hat pulled down and his raincoat collar turned up against the rain, she would not have seen his face if, just as he passed under a station light, the engineer had not let off steam. The figure in the raincoat jumped and Denis perceived that it was Jarret.

Puzzled and disturbed, she returned to her own seat. La Baie was two stations before her own she noted, on consulting the timetable, which meant that it was three stations before Trois Lacs. Why had Jarret bought a ticket to Trois Lacs if he was getting off at La Baie? Was he suspicious that she would not keep her unspoken but tacit promise not to give him away? Or could she have said something that made him change his mind?

She had asked about the country around Laurentville and

he had been enthusiastic about it. That was encouraging. He knew something of *Manoir Laurent*, too, Denis was convinced. But why, when he had a ticket for somewhere else, did Jarret get off at La Baie? Or had that been his intention all along?

The conductor passed through the car to collect the tickets of passengers who would get off at the next station and Denis suddenly noticed that Jarret had forgotten to take the ticket receipt that identified him as a Trois Lacs passenger. It remained where the conductor had stuck it, in the back of the seat ahead along with her own. Denis was still gazing thoughtfully at the small piece of pasteboard with the penciled number when the train stopped at the next station.

Finally, after a long pause, it got under way again. Impulsively Denis stood up to put on her coat and before she sat down had taken possession of the receipt Jarret had left. It was clutched in one tightly closed hand when the conductor picked up her own ticket receipt. After he left the car she looked around guiltily, hesitated and then opened her purse and slid the scrap of pasteboard deep into its zipper compartment. Right or wrong, she had given a tacit promise and if that were possible, intended to keep it.

CHAPTER II

The Portrait

AT LAURENTVILLE it was raining harder than ever. Water streamed off the conductor's helmet as he reached for her suitcase and helped Denis down the steps of the train. The wind blew a wet strand of hair across her eyes so that when someone grabbed the suitcase, caught her by the arm and rushed her down the platform, Denis knew it was Uncle Guy only by his voice.

"Looks as though we were trying to drown you. But how we needed this rain! Here's the car. Pop in."

He opened the door of the back seat, Denis jumped in and he pushed the suitcase in after her before he slammed the door and slid into the driver's seat ahead.

"A wet welcome, eh, Denis? But your trunk came yesterday so all we have to do is pick up Clem and Midge at the store and head straight for home and supper."

He had started the car and they were soon driving through the main street of what seemed to be a small town. Dimly the lights of a few stores showed through the rain. When Uncle Guy stopped before one of them and honked his horn, someone ran out with a box of groceries. Denis could hear it being stored away in the back. Then the front door was pulled open and a voice shouted above the noise of the motor and the wind.

"Bernard gave Midge a chipmunk. I've done my best, Dad, but she won't come without it."

There was an impatient ejaculation from Uncle Guy before he shut off the motor. "Get in, Clem. I'll attend to Midge. And you may as well drive," he added before he opened his own door, ran around the front of the car and disappeared into the store.

All Denis could see of Clem as he slid under the wheel was that he was big, even taller than his father. He was chuckling to himself. "I'll bet on Midge," he remarked, then turned, stretched out a long arm and switched on the light.

"Hi, Denis! Let's have a look at you."

Denis blinked resentfully against the suddenness of the light before she considered the face turned to hers. It was a long face and homely, with an aggressive chin the prominent feature. His hair, what she could see of it, was—yes, it was red. And two very blue eyes scanned her with an impudent directness.

Disconcerted by their scrutiny, Denis could only summon a lofty, "Well?"

Whereupon Clem's mouth took on a humorous twist. What a provoking boy! Why, he wasn't too much older than she was and he was laughing at her. Denis clutched at the thought that she was going to be a concert pianist and tried to assume the air of one.

But Clem only remarked, "Well, they didn't name you after your grandfather because you look like him, did they? Here comes Dad with Midge."

The door of the back seat opened and a small figure in a raincape was ushered in. Under the hood of the cape Denis caught a glimpse of two blond braids and a row of freckles across an absurdly small nose. Then Uncle Guy snapped off the light, joined Clem in front and said in a resigned way that they had better get started.

"She has it, I suppose," said Clem.

"Yes. And I don't know what Felice will say." The older man sounded impatient. He turned his head. "Your mother probably won't let you keep that chipmunk, you know, Midge."

When there was no response from the small figure huddled in the far corner of the back seat, he added quickly, "Have you greeted your cousin Denis?"

"How do you do, Cousin Denis?" a soft little voice said politely.

The town lights were left behind now and through the darkness and rain all that could be seen was the wet ribbon of road ahead as the headlights of the car picked it up.

After a silence Uncle Guy said anxiously, "Her mother won't have it, Clem."

"I'm afraid not," said Clem.

His tone and that of his father presented Aunt Felice as a kind of martinet and the prospect was not reassuring to Denis. She had already decided that she did not like Clem. Instinctively she moved closer to the child in the opposite corner.

"Whatever possessed Bernard to give it to her?" Uncle Guy grumbled presently.

From the depths of the raincape Midge explained briefly, "He's lame."

Her father had no answer to that and there was another silence. Then Clem turned into a side road and as the car bumped over a bad stretch Denis heard small sounds from the opposite corner, soft chirps of comfort. She moved still closer to Midge.

"Is he frightened?" she whispered sympathetically.

The child edged out of her corner so that they were sitting side by side. "It's only the car. He's tame," she confided.

"Do we have much farther to go?" whispered Denis as they turned again and the car bumped and swayed.

"No, this is our road," Midge said between coos of reassurance into her cape.

They stopped at last, at a stone house with a long, narrow, covered gallery. The door opened and a boy Clem called Jeanpierre said something in French as he took the bag, while a young girl drew Denis inside.

"Here you are at last. Are you soaked? Let me take your coat. I'm Claire," she said all in one breath and gave Denis a little squeeze of welcome.

Her simple directness was engaging and although Claire was a few years older, Denis knew at once that she was going to like her, that they would get on. Clem had gone off with the car, Uncle Guy was stripping off his wet raincoat and Midge was shedding hers.

"You've had a long journey and then all this rain. But we have a fire. Come in and see Mamma before——" Claire stopped as her small sister finally emerged from the raincape and the chipmunk was revealed.

"Oh, Midge! Not another?" Claire moaned.

"She would bring it," said Uncle Guy.

"But Mamma——" Claire looked at him helplessly.

"I know. But go along, we may as well get the verdict over." He waved them through a wide doorway into the living room.

Opposite the door, at the far end of the room, Denis saw the fire. Her first confused impression was of the fireplace, with a large portrait hanging above the mantel and of the woman and young girl who stood before the fire. Then she was aware of the grace of the woman with prematurely grey hair who advanced to greet her.

Aunt Felice was slender, with an assured dignity, a gracious manner and that illusive quality, charm. Although she was nothing like the voluble, domineering Frenchwoman Denis had expected, there could not be the slightest doubt who ruled at *Manoir Laurent*. She had a low and beautifully modulated voice but spoke rapidly and with authority.

"Denise, my child, I am most happy to see you. Your train was late, yes? You are hungry? And chilled no doubt. Come to the fire."

The portrait over the mantel, Denis saw a moment later, was that of her grandfather Denis Laurent, as he called himself professionally. One of the hands that played the piano so brilliantly all the world wanted to hear him, rested on the arm of a chair and Denis, always interested in hands, noted it with pride. She was surprised to see a large gold ring on the little finger. The picture had been painted before his hair turned grey but the black eyes she remembered so well

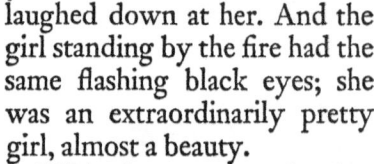

laughed down at her. And the girl standing by the fire had the same flashing black eyes; she was an extraordinarily pretty girl, almost a beauty.

"This is your cousin Angelica, Denise," said the older woman.

"It is Denis, my dear," Uncle Guy corrected. "Not Denise. Lawrence named his daughter after Father."

"Certainly. But she is a girl, therefore she is Denise," Aunt Felice decided.

Meanwhile Angelica, who could be only about fifteen, although her cool self-possession made her seem older than Claire, greeted Denis politely. Then her expression changed, the black eyes widened dramatically.

"*Mais regardez cette enfant*," she cried, pointing at Midge. "Oh, I forgot. I am to speak

English because of Denis. But Mamma, look! It's a rat this time."

"It's not a rat," Midge objected passionately. It's a young chipmunk."

"What's the difference? A rat!" Angelica shuddered fastidiously. "Make her put it out."

Aunt Felice had turned and was surveying her youngest with a baffled look of annoyance. Eyebrows raised in disapproval, she glanced at Uncle Guy.

"Bernard Papineau gave it to her," he explained ruefully. "I did my best to persuade Midge not to bring it."

Aunt Felice frowned at her youngest daughter. "I told you there were to be no more pets, Margot," she said quietly.

"I should think not," cried Angelica. "It's bad enough to have a cat and two dogs and a lamb and a calf, to say nothing of that awful crow, following Midge into the house. Without a rat, a horrid——"

"He's not a rat," Midge protested. Her head, with its rumpled blond braids, was bent protectively over the chipmunk, held in the crook of her arm. Suddenly he ran up and sat on her shoulder. Whereupon the big black poodle and the cocker who had just raced into the living room flung themselves at Midge only to sit back obediently at her soft word of command. The chipmunk peered at them curiously, quite unperturbed by Angelica's shriek of protest.

"A horrid little rat," she shuddered. "Make Midge put it——"

Aunt Felice silenced her with a gesture before she said—and her tone was final, "The chipmunk must go back to the woods, Margot."

Fascinated by its confidence in Midge, Denis had been watching the small animal. She saw a quiver go through the child before, undaunted, Midge looked straight at her mother and ventured to appeal the decision.

"He is so young. And lame. How could he live in the woods?"

Her mother frowned. "Then he must go back to Bernard Papineau. You forget, *n'est-ce pas*, that beginning next week you go each day to school at the convent. Who would care for him? We are too busy here to look after any more pets."

There was a silence. Claire opened her mouth only to close it helplessly, and Uncle Guy cleared his throat but did not speak. Angelica smiled triumphantly. Midge looked down, then suddenly raised her head and gazed at the portrait of her grandfather in earnest appeal.

One by one the others followed her glance and Denis was startled to discover how lifelike the picture was. The amused black eyes of Denis Laurent seemed to prompt, "Courage, speak up! I did, you know. Remember the kitten?"

Denis took a deep breath and surprised herself. "I'll look after the chipmunk while Midge is in school, Aunt Felice. I'd like to. Please let me."

Midge's surprised look of gratitude was reward for her daring. It enabled Denis to ignore Angelica's baleful glance and face Aunt Felice expectantly.

The older woman's face wore an inscrutable expression. She surveyed her niece without speaking but Uncle Guy said heartily that it was a good idea. Denis would feel more at home if she had something to do, he told his wife.

"It will not be difficult to give Denise things to do," Aunt Felice remarked dryly. But she glanced at the portrait again and finally agreed with a resigned shake of her head, *"Eh bien*, Margot. You may keep the small chipmunk until he grows up or can take care of himself. But he must be the last, you understand?"

"*Oui*, Mamma," Midge said demurely.

"*Eh bien.* Now run along and put him in a cage and get washed for supper."

Angelica sniffed contemptuously, "A rat! Grandfather bewitches you all, even when he's not here," she grumbled and made a face at the portrait.

But only Denis noticed because the others were watching Midge as she walked the length of the room, murmuring to the animal on her shoulder and followed by the two dogs. Aunt Felice wore the same puzzled, slightly baffled look Denis had noticed before but Uncle Guy and Claire were smiling affectionately.

"They seem to understand each other. Midge has an uncanny way with animals," said Uncle Guy. "Just as her grandfather has. Oh, by the by, I had a letter from Father today."

Aunt Felice turned with interest, "Yes?"

"He is coming home?" Claire asked eagerly.

But there was an exaggerated groan from Angelica. "He'll probably bring a panda and—and what's that other thing—a platypus and——" She stopped at a word from her mother but she continued to glare at the portrait.

"Is it true, Guy? Your father comes home at last?" Aunt Felice asked.

"He didn't say. He is in New Zealand."

"New Zealand? And only a few weeks ago it was Australia. And before that came a letter from South Africa. *Pourquoi?* He does not give the concerts. Or does he, perhaps?" Aunt Felice added thoughtfully.

"No, there have been no concert engagements for nearly a year, we can be sure of that. And his agent here is impatient because Father does not even respond to communications urging him to return. I don't understand it," Uncle Guy added and looked at the painting as though to find an answer there.

Again they all followed suit, and Denis mentioned the ring. She was not surprised when Uncle Guy said it was a family ring from the Laurent side of the family, that his father had only worn it to please the artist. To Denis her grandfather seemed to take on a mischievous air. It was as though he cherished some amusing secret and challenged them to guess it. And so excellent was the portrait, so living its handsome, debonair subject that Denis would not have been in the least surprised had he winked at her.

Uncle Guy's puzzled look faded, Claire was smiling and on Aunt Felice's face there was a look of amused affection.

"It is that we miss him," she said and added wisely, "No doubt your father travels to enjoy a rest from music."

"And to collect some more animals," Angelica muttered.

There was a chuckle from Clem who had come in unnoticed and was standing behind them. "You know you'll be as glad as the rest of us to see Grandfather, Angie. Even if he brings a dozen monkeys."

"Let us pray he brings only himself," said Aunt Felice. "But we forget that Denise has just arrived. You must be hungry, my dear. You would like to go to your room? No? Then we will have supper." With a characteristic gesture of one hand she made it, however gracious, a command.

Claire hurried ahead in search of Midge and Uncle Guy strode after his wife while Denis, to her surprise, found Angelica's arm slipped companionably through hers. The younger girl appeared to have forgotten the chipmunk incident, although there was a secret look of mischief in the black eyes.

"I hope there is something very special for supper, don't you?" Angelica said gaily.

"She means something sweet," said Clem.

"How right you are," his sister retorted.

"An expression much used by a certain boy from the States who visited in Laurentville this summer," Clem pointed out. "It was about all he could say, wasn't it, Angie?"

"That's what you think," she returned, but laughed when Clem whistled in derision.

"Gosh, Angie, you never told me he had two expressions."

Denis was only half listening because she was surreptitiously inspecting the big room, so unlike that at home. It was not only the beautiful old chests, their polished wood shining in the lamplight, or the deeply recessed windows or the lovely feeling of space that impressed her. Everything was spotless and beautifully ordered; nothing was shabby, but nothing was new. Everything had a beauty that even Denis recognized as the mellowness of age. It was as though people had always used the tables, walked on the rugs and sat in the chairs and always would. She never had lived in a room like that.

In the corner at the left of the door was a grand piano. And when, just before they reached it, a large grey Persian cat slid around the door jamb and streaked off under the piano, Denis stopped short, with an involuntary exclamation, then hastened to avert her gaze and move on.

"What's the matter?" said Clem. "That was only Muff. Don't you like cats?"

But Angelica was quicker. "It's the piano, isn't it, Denis? Father said you would not even look at one."

Denis did not contradict her. It was not the piano, however, nor was it the cat. What had startled her was one of the framed photographs that stood on the piano, a photograph large enough so that there was no mistaking it to be the boy on the train—Jarret.

CHAPTER III

A Telephone Call

AT THE long table in the dining room Denis found herself between Claire and Angelica, with Clem and Midge opposite. Since she and her mother usually had their dinner on a card table, or more often than not she had to eat alone because Mrs. Fraser was away on business or dining with a client, it seemed strange and partyish to have supper with such a large family. And there was a Frenchwoman in the kitchen, a cat in the living room, a chipmunk somewhere upstairs and two dogs watching from the hall.

Apparently not permitted beyond the threshold, the Cocker Spaniel, Charcoal, lay with his chin on the sill and his silky ears spread over it, his brown eyes wistful but resigned. Beside him sat a big black Poodle looking less philosophical.

"Nicolette really belongs to Grandfather, and she's spoiled," Claire explained.

Denis smiled politely. She thought both dogs very good, but her mind was on the photograph in the other room. Who was Jarret? She watched Uncle Guy carve a ham at one end of the table, while Aunt Felice poured chocolate at the other, and thought of the photograph. She jumped at the sound of her own name.

Angelica was asking curiously, "Did they name you after Grandfather so you'd be a pianist? Or was it the other way around? Do you like having a boy's name?"

Because the name had been her father's choice, Denis stiffened indignantly when Clem answered the question for her.

"Of course she doesn't. And Denise is too French. Let's call her Dee. That's feminine."

"And loving," Midge said unexpectedly and with such sober approval that everybody laughed.

But when Denis smiled in pleased surprise at the child across the table, Clem murmured, "You ought to smile oftener, Brown Eyes."

Although she wanted to retort that he was not very original, Denis pretended not to hear. She was far from sure she liked Clem, yet uncertain what to do about him. She was wary of Angelica, too. There was a secret look of mischief in the younger girl's black eyes and they missed nothing. Claire, on the other hand, was comfortably like Uncle Guy. And Midge was a darling.

Denis ignored Clem and smiled again at Midge. "What are you going to name the chipmunk?" she asked.

Midge was uncertain. She had thought of calling him Skipper or maybe Napoleon. She had just indicated her willingness to listen to suggestions when Curly Rose appeared in the doorway and announced that there was a telephone call from Montreal.

Aunt Felice said it must be for her, that she was expecting a call from her sister. She left the room, Claire took over the pouring of the chocolate and they returned to the question of a name for the chipmunk.

Clem said why not call him Chippy? Or she might name him after a *coureur de bois;* a chipmunk certainly was a runner

of the woods. Claire stood out for Monsieur Brown because of his color and Angelica said no matter what they called him he would still be Rat to her.

"I'll call him Mr. Chip," Midge decided.

Then Aunt Felice came back and the chipmunk was forgotten when she told Uncle Guy gravely, "Your brother Duncan wishes to talk with you. Jarret has run away."

"Run away!" Uncle Guy put down his carving knife and went off to the telephone, leaving Aunt Felice to take his place at the ham.

Denis, who felt as though guilty knowledge must be written all over her, drew a relieved breath when she discovered that no one was paying her the slightest attention. They all looked expectantly at Aunt Felice and there was an incredulous silence before, simultaneously, Clem whistled and Angelica giggled.

"What fun!" said Angelica.

"But, why?" Claire said in a puzzled tone. "Why did Jarret do that?"

Midge opened her mouth, then closed it tight and looked at her plate.

Clem started to say something but changed his mind.

Nervously Denis stammered, "Who is—Jarret?"

They all, even Midge, surveyed her in amazement. Then Angelica giggled again. "So that's all Canadian cousins mean in the States."

Denis flushed and Aunt Felice said quickly, "I remember now, Denise. Your father did not get on with his other brother. No doubt that is why you have not heard of Jarret. He is your uncle Duncan's son."

So that pompous little man she had seen at Côte L'Avenir was her own uncle. No wonder her father did not get on with him, thought Denis.

"Jarret is your cousin, just as we are," Claire was saying.

"All but Clem," Angelica murmured slyly.

"She means I'm adopted," Clem explained simply.

Then Uncle Guy came back and had to face an instant

barrage of questions. Had Jarret really run away? Why? Was his father upset? When did it happen?

The discovery that the boy on the train was her own cousin had given Denis so much to think about that she did not hear all the questions. What would she have done had she known? No wonder Jarret had been startled when she told him she was visiting cousins at *Manoir Laurent*. And Clem! Clem was no relation actually. Now she understood the red hair and the fact that he did not resemble the others. She was surreptitiously inspecting him when Claire asked the question that put her on guard.

"When did it happen? I thought Jarret was off to college," said Claire.

Denis tried her best to seem unconcerned as she waited for the response but she was thankful Clem was not watching her.

Uncle Guy had lifted a hand for silence and now he explained that Jarret was in fact on the way to college. His father had decided to go with him as far as Montreal and they had driven to Côte L'Avenir to catch the express. They were scarcely on board when Jarret discovered that he had left a package in the waiting room and while the train took water had jumped off to get it. He never got on again.

"Good for Jarret," muttered Angelica. "What a tizzy Uncle Duncan will be in!"

Sternly and in French Aunt Felice ordered her to be quiet.

His father had assumed that Jarret returned to the train through another car, Uncle Guy pointed out. When he did not appear and a search of the train showed that he was not on it, Duncan was frantic. He had wired Côte L'Avenir from the first stop.

"Jarret was not there but the station agent came back with the suggestion that he might have taken the local by mistake and—— By Jove! That was your train, Denis. Did you see a man and a boy at Côte L'Avenir? Did the boy get on the local?"

Although Denis had been waiting for some such question, now that it had come she was so afraid she might unwittingly give Jarret away that she was suddenly in a panic. Under the scrutiny of Clem's keen blue eyes she squeezed her handkerchief in cold fingers and tried desperately to look innocent.

"Yes, I did see a man and a boy," she admitted carefully. "They walked up and down the platform until the express came." Denis hesitated, hoping she did not look as guilty as she felt, and finally added that the boy seemed to be arguing with his father about something.

Uncle Guy thought there was no doubt the two were his brother and nephew. The boy was not anxious to go to college, it seemed, and may have been putting up a last plea. The question was whether he had boarded the local train. Or had something happened to him?

Hastily Denis crossed her fingers, determined to fib if necessary rather than give Jarret away. Nothing could have happened to him surely. Yet she was faintly alarmed to learn that he had not notified his father of his safety as agreed.

"You didn't see the boy get on your train?" said Uncle Guy.

Denis relaxed, thankful she could reply truthfully, "No, I didn't."

"But that doesn't say he was not on it," said Clem. "Why should he stay at Côte L'Avenir? Isn't it more likely, Dad, that he was coming back to us?"

"That is what Duncan thought might have happened," said Uncle Guy. "I had to tell him no one but Denis got off the train at Laurentville. I'll have something to eat and then make a few telephone calls. That is about all we can do tonight."

While Uncle Guy ate his supper they talked about Jarret. His father owned an asbestos mine at Wickham Vale, it appeared, but Jarret usually spent his summers at *Manoir Laurent* and had only gone home two weeks ago in order to get ready for college. He was to major in engineering at a college in the States and according to his father the boy was suddenly not anxious to go.

"He should have told Uncle Duncan he wouldn't go," said Angie.

"Told Uncle Duncan?" Claire raised her eyebrows incredulously.

Even Uncle Guy agreed that would be impossible.

Clem said slowly, "I can't quite picture Jarret as a mining engineer, it's true, but surely he wouldn't run away just because he had suddenly decided he didn't want to go to college. Perhaps there was something else he——" Clem broke off, his eyes drawn together in a thoughtful frown as he went on eating his supper.

Denis took no further part in the conversation but occupied herself with her food. She was disquieted by the fact that Jarret had not kept his promise to notify his father that he was safe. Suppose something had happened to him at La Baie? She alone knew that he got off there. Then it occurred to her that if Jarret wrote his father a letter the older man could not possibly get it until tomorrow or possibly the next day.

Uncle Guy was greatly disturbed. If the boy had run away where could he have gone? And if not, what had happened to him? It was unfortunate that Duncan always wanted things his own way, never could seem to understand the other fellow's point of view.

"Duncan couldn't understand why Lawrence wanted to be an actor, and did everything he could to prevent it. So Larry went off to the States and never came back. Now it's Jarret." Uncle Guy swallowed the last of his chocolate, wiped his mouth with his napkin and stood up. No, he would not have any dessert, he wanted to get a call in.

He went off to the telephone leaving them to the exciting discussion of whether Jarret had run away and where he could be. Aunt Felice was perturbed, Claire incredulous, Clem puzzled and Angelica delighted. Midge alone said nothing. Denis, who thought she never had tasted anything more delicious than the rolled French pancakes filled with raspberry jam which were served for dessert, listened to the others and watched Midge. Now that she knew more of Uncle Duncan she did not wonder Jarret had run away and was glad to keep his secret. Imagine that cocky little man trying to keep her father from going on the stage!

Jarret, it seemed, had been at *Manoir Laurent* all summer. He had worked on the farm and fished and tramped through the woods he loved. On the subject of college he had said little except that he was going. Clem insisted that was not strange since Jarret never had talked much, except to Midge or his grandfather.

"I wish Grandfather were here," Angelica said gleefully. "He'd love the idea of Jarret doing a skip. He thinks Uncle Duncan is stuffy, you know he does."

Aunt Felice reproved her sternly in French, adding, "*Et qu'est-ce que c'est* 'doing a skeep'? It sounds a rude expression. Where do you learn such things?"

"That boy from the States again," said Clem with a chuckle. "He had more of a vocabulary than I thought. But seriously it is a pity Grandfather isn't here. He always understood Jarret better than anyone else."

Denis had finished her own pancakes and was watching Midge relish the last of hers. She was not surprised to see the child repress a smile and it added to her suspicion that Midge knew or guessed why Jarret had run away even if she did not know where he was.

Aunt Felice had agreed that it was indeed unfortunate their grandfather was not there and had then closed the discussion by saying that until they knew more it was useless to talk.

Angelica promptly turned to Denis. "If my father had been an actor I'd want to go on the stage, too. Didn't you ever want to be an actress?"

Denis hesitated, loath to have Angelica know how much she had wanted to be like her father. She must have been about ten when she announced that she was going to be an actress and was told never to mention the subject again. Even if, in relating something that had happened at school, she imitated one of the teachers or another girl, Mrs. Fraser stopped her immediately. And there was always some good reason why

Denis must not take any part in the school plays. Fearful she had inherited Larry Fraser's love of the stage, her mother was determined Denis should not follow his profession. She was to be a pianist like her grandfather.

"Why aren't you going to be an actress?" Angelica persisted.

"Because I am going to be a concert pianist," Denis told her stiffly and heard an unmistakable chuckle from across the table.

"A pianist who won't touch a piano?" Clem teased. "But maybe you are something of an actress anyway, eh?"

What did he mean by that? Did he suspect she had seen Jarret on the train? Denis was thankful when Aunt Felice rose saying it was late, long past Midge's bedtime, and no doubt Denise was tired after her journey and would like to go to her room.

Denis, suddenly overcome by the strangeness of everything, admitted gratefully that she would. Coming into a large family was rather like a dive into icy water; it stunned you temporarily so you couldn't think at all, much less quickly. She said goodnight and followed Claire and Midge upstairs, thankful to be away from Angelica's curious questions, from Clem's shrewd appraisal. It would never do to let him grill her on the subject of Jarret tonight.

She did not like what she had heard about her father's other brother. For a moment at Côte L'Avenir she had felt sorry for the pompous little man who had turned out to be her own uncle. But now that she knew Duncan Fraser had tried to keep her father from the profession he loved, Denis felt something like an active dislike for him. Now she was glad Jarret had run away. And Clem-the-Suspicious needn't think he could worm anything out of her.

Too sleepy to unpack more than the necessary things for the night, she was comforted by her room. The walls were blue and the simple furniture was painted a soft buff yellow; the curtains were very crisp and white, and best of all, there was a small fireplace. What fun, what utter luxury to have an open fire in your room on cold mornings. As she brushed her hair, yawned and tumbled into bed, Denis felt as though she had walked into some story of another day. She must keep Jarret's secret in spite of Clem. Was it because he was adopted that Clem called Aunt Felice "Ma Tante" instead of the French Mam-ma as the others did, she wondered, yawned again and fell asleep.

CHAPTER IV

A Week Later

THE WEATHER was warm for September and the windows were open; a gentle wind fluttered the curtains and brought the warm, crusty odor of baking bread up from the kitchens below. The hum of a tractor in the field where they were cutting oats, the occasional bark of a dog and a snatch of song came with them. After Denis finished making the bed as Claire had showed her Aunt Felice liked it to be made, sheets drawn taut and hospital corners folded neatly under, she drifted over to the window.

The field of oats was like a sea of gold, stirred by the wind into lazy waves. The strip of white beyond was buckwheat, she had learned, and beyond the buckwheat were more oats, cut and stacked into golden sheaves. But for her illness, she would be at the music school now and later in the day at home, practicing. Denis shuddered away from the prospect. She didn't want to sit at a piano all day, she thought passionately; she wanted to do the things other girls did. But if she was going to be a pianist, as of course she was—— Oh, everything was so mixed up. She had only been at *Manoir Laurent* a week, yet already she felt a different person. It seemed disloyal to her mother and her music but—— "But I love being here," Denis admitted to her secret self.

It was fun being part of a large family where something happened all the time. Yes, she was going to be a pianist some day, of course she was. Meanwhile it was exciting just to be alive. One of the habitant farm hands passed below the window singing a native air and Denis found her foot tapping out its rhythm.

"Are you there, Dee?"

She turned and saw Midge's head, with its honey-colored

pigtails, appear around the door. Was Mr. Chip there, the child was anxious to know.

"He was a few minutes ago," said Denis. "He was trying to get into my knitting bag."

Midge had some dry cereal and beech nuts for her pet and wanted to know if Dee would feed him since she was going to fish in the brook.

When Denis agreed to see that Mr. Chip got his food, Midge thanked her, left the nuts and started off. She had been in school at the convent each day for a week and the outdoors was beckoning.

Denis called her back. "Wait a minute. I've been wondering," she began slowly. "Jarret liked to fish, I've heard. Do you suppose he is in the mountains somewhere, fishing?" She flicked a hand in what was supposed to be the direction of the Laurentians.

Midge's face had taken on a blank expression. "I don't know," was her only response but it came immediately.

"But you know why he ran away, don't you?" Denis asked quickly and was rewarded by the child's hesitation; her weight shifted from one foot to the other and she did not reply.

The boy on the train had said, "Not until I've tried——" Tried what, Denis wondered. Did Midge know? But if she did she had no intention of saying, for her lips were suddenly pressed tightly together. Jarret's secret, whatever it was, would be safe with Midge; her only response was a slight shrug.

To Denis it was a matter of curiosity more than anything else now because a message had finally reached Uncle Duncan. It had come in the shape of a telegram taken over the telephone by his cook the night Jarret disappeared. The French-woman knew nothing of what had happened and since she was in a hurry to close the house and get off for a few days she had scrawled it on the back of a letter. Thus it was not until Duncan Fraser reached home two days later that he found the message with his other mail. It read: "Don't worry everything all right—Jarret."

Uncle Duncan had no way of knowing where the wire had come from, but Côte L'Avenir and all the nearby villages had been combed for the boy without finding a trace of him.

Presumably he had telegraphed from La Baie, but with the ticket to Trois Lacs safely tucked away in her purse, Denis was convinced that La Baie was not Jarret's real destination. Why Trois Lacs? What did Jarret propose to do, or try to do, there? Whatever it was, she was now definitely on his side because the more she learned about Uncle Duncan the less she liked him.

Denis turned away from the window at last and began to dust. The chipmunk was scampering happily about, poking his curious nose into everything. When she came to the chest of drawers Denis found him sitting up on the top of it with a lipstick clutched between his tiny hands.

"I'm afraid that won't be of any use to you, Mr. Chip," said Denis, laughing.

Evidently the chipmunk had reached the same conclusion since he willingly exchanged it for the food she offered, most of which he stuffed into his cheek pouches before he ran up her arm and sat on her shoulder, eating a nut while she finished dusting.

"You make me hungry," said Denis and moved back to the window for another sniff of the fresh bread, French bread probably that would be brown and crusty on the outside, feathery white within. There was a new odor mingled with it now. Apple pie, perhaps? Claire and Aunt Felice were both in the kitchen with Curly Rose this morning, so all sorts of good things must be in the making. Aunt Felice looked upon cooking as an art, to be practiced with loving skill, and she was training Claire to that goal. I wish Claire would teach me to cook, thought Denis.

She felt more comfortable with Claire than with Aunt Felice although the Frenchwoman's gracious manner and lovely voice fascinated her. The trouble was that Aunt Felice was so clever and quick she made one feel awkward. Midge alone could fluster her mother. The child's inability to remember that calves, birds, grasshoppers and the rest were not welcome in the house not only annoyed but seemed to baffle Aunt Felice.

"What are you doing now?" said Denis as the chipmunk ran down her arm and onto the window sill where he sat up and nosed something he held between his little hands. Because of his lameness he was extraordinarily tame and had become a general pet. Clem had made him a nest in a wire-covered box in Midge's room to which Mr. Chip added all sorts of treasures from nuts and their shells to bits of wool. According to Uncle Guy, he might curl up there and sleep through the cold months. Chipmunks lived underground and presumably hibernated most of the winter. Meanwhile he was so clean that he had the run of the house.

"What have you there? Why, you wretch, it's one of the wool flowers off my dress," Denis cried suddenly and pounced.

This was a mistake because it frightened her quarry who promptly bounded down out of reach. And it proved useless to chase him about the room since he was so much quicker than she and thought it a fine game. After wasting ten minutes in a futile effort to capture him, Denis sat down and rattled the contents of her sewing box until Mr. Chip's curiosity proved too strong. He hastily buried his prize between her pillows and darted over to investigate.

Denis gave him another nut and recovered the wool flower. Unfortunately she left her sewing box open on the chair while she did so and Mr. Chip poked his inquisitive nose into it, upsetting the box. His look of surprise before he scurried off in a fright turned her moan of dismay to a giggle. But while she crawled about the floor after rolling spools and buttons and pins, the chipmunk recovered his confidence, joined in the hunt and had soon captured a thimble. She was scarcely seated before he was up on her knee with it.

Denis quietly closed the workbox, and having learned her lesson, reached forward without haste and took the sleek, furry brown animal between her two hands.

"You inquisitive little pest," she said affectionately.

44

The bright eyes looked back at her undaunted and the wee nose sniffed curiously before Mr. Chip slipped out of her grasp and jumped to the window sill where he sat up and chattered at her impudently—"Cuk-cuk!"

Uhmm! Whatever was cooking must be simply super. Denis leaned her elbows on the sill and indulged in a long whiff while her gaze roamed admiringly over the country spread out below. How different from the outlook at home! In the Ohio city from which she had come, their frame house was built on a narrow lot like the many others around it, so that backyards with the inevitable laundry, or a street lined with small lawns, made the only view.

The golden field of oats, the woods sweeping toward the mysteriously blue mountains, suddenly drew Denis like a great magnet. She would write her letter to her mother on the sunny gallery along the back of the house. Hadn't she been told to stay out-of-doors?

She caught up a writing pad and her pen and after leaving Mr. Chip in Midge's room, went downstairs. She would have liked to go down through the kitchen in the hope of being invited to sample a piece of whatever that smell was, or maybe a fresh roll. But instinct told her she would not be welcomed by Aunt Felice. Denis went down the front way and out the door at the rear of the hall.

The back gallery, like that along the front of the house, was less than four feet wide and close to the ground, more like a terrace. Like the front, however, it was included under the steeply pitched roof of the house itself and ran the full width of the building. It overlooked a sweep of country similar to that in front except that here was the stone root house and beyond it the old stone barn; here the fields sloped gently to a brook.

In the distance the silvery steeple of a church, rising from a huddle of buildings, indicated a village. A puff of smoke appeared above the woodland to the east—or was it west—just before a train, so small in the distance as to seem a mere toy, emerged from the woods. Denis watched it snake its way

across the valley, shivering with pleasure at its lonely wail when it whistled a crossing, before she began her letter.

Everything was so different, she told her mother. Just living in the country seemed strange. There were few English people in Laurentville or in the country about; she heard French spoken constantly. The habitants, like Jeanpierre and Poleon Dulac, who worked with and for Uncle Guy jabbered in a kind of patois and so did Curly Rose who helped in the kitchen. Although Aunt Felice was careful to speak only English when Denis was present, Angelica and even Midge often lapsed into French.

Denis paused, partly because she was thinking of Angelica. She had been relieved when the younger girl went off to boarding school two or three days after her arrival. It was bad enough to have to cope with Clem's teasing, get used to Claire's grown-up ability and overcome her awe of Aunt Felice without having to deal with Angelica's sharp eyes and candid tongue. To be sure the boarding school was only fifty miles away and Angelica would often come home over week ends but by that time Denis would be more at home.

Someone was singing again. It was Jeanpierre, she discovered, as he came around the corner of the house on his way to the barn. He had a good voice and sang with youthful vigor and enjoyment; he reminded her of Jarret somehow, although he was older.

Denis could understand only a word or two of his song—something about *boule roulant*—but the air was tuneful and had a gay swing. Unconsciously she hummed it, too, wishing she knew the words. Then Jeanpierre disappeared into the barn and she was about to resume her writing when Midge came flying up from the brook pursued by Charcoal.

The Cocker's long ears spread out as he ran and Midge's pigtails flapped. She reached the house first, bounded onto the gallery and the screen door banged behind her as she disappeared into the house, leaving Charcoal to sit panting outside.

Almost immediately there was a small explosion in the hall. This was followed by a startled cry of protest from Aunt Felice, a scramble and a patter of French. Then the screen door was flung open and something tossed out, a small leggy thing that landed in the grass, righted itself and hopped.

"*Mais Mam-ma! Ma grenouille*," shrieked Midge and at the frog's first leap was out the door and after it, aided by Charcoal.

"Margot!"

"My frog, Mamma! *Ma grenouille!*" Midge's voice came back faintly as she and Charcoal pursued the frog under the fence into the next field and out of sight.

Aunt Felice, with the frustrated look that Midge always seemed to bring to her face, stood in the doorway and shook her head at Denis. It was all very well for Margot to say she had not intended to bring the frog inside, that he had merely happened to be in her pocket and got out while she rummaged in the closet for her fishing boots. But *une petite fille!* And a frog!

47

"A little girl! Why should a little girl want to have a frog in her pocket?" the older woman demanded with a shudder of distaste. "Frogs are good to eat, yes, but not to pet." Margot would have to be punished; she must learn not to bring her odd companions indoors. Meanwhile perhaps Denis would take the brioche to her uncle and Clem. At this hour in the morning Poleon took them milk and they liked something to eat with it, the older woman explained, adding, "There is one for you as well, Denise."

Denis nibbled the warm brioche hungrily as she crossed the field. She seemed to be hungry all the time here, and like everything else that came from Aunt Felice's kitchen, the brioche was simply scrumptious. In fact she had had more good things to eat in the past week than in all the rest of her life. It must be wonderful to be able to cook things like this.

Her uncle and Clem stood in the shade of the maple at the corner of the field talking with Poleon Dulac. Uncle Guy ate his brioche at once and went off to the barn with the Frenchman but Clem leaned against the fence for a leisurely savoring of his.

"Good, eh? No one can cook like Ma Tante. Has she been giving you a lesson?"

When Denis shook her head his eyebrows went up. "What? Idling away a Saturday morning?"

Denis bristled. She had not been idle of course but he shouldn't have the satisfaction of knowing it. In her most aloof, going-to-be-a-concert-pianist manner, she agreed thoughtfully that she supposed she was wasting her time. But the doctor had said she must not practice yet and——

"And you don't want to, anyway," Clem finished. "What's so important about being a pianist?" he demanded. With a challenging twinkle in the blue eyes and apparently oblivious of the anger boiling up in Denis, he added, "See that old Frenchman talking to Dad and Poleon over by the barn? He's the finest gardener for miles around, raises the best vegetables. In his line he's an artist, as important as Grandfather. You should get over the idea that music sets you apart."

"Must you be rude?" Denis said icily.

Clem looked at her in surprise before an angry frown drew his eyes together.

"Rude?" He laughed shortly. "Golly! You sound like Uncle Duncan."

"Uncle Duncan! Uncle Duncan!" Denis blazed. "Don't you dare compare me to him. I don't blame Jarret for running away."

Clem's annoyance faded and a slow, exasperating grin wiped out the frown. "No? Is that why you said you didn't see him on the train?"

Denis stood mute, at loss for a safe retort. Then anger overcame caution and she sputtered furiously, "Is it the red hair that makes you so impossible or—or—— Why anyone ever adopted you I cannot imagine," she flung at him and stalked off, only to stop after a dozen steps and look over her shoulder.

"I told you I did not see Jarret get on the train," Denis pointed out with dignity in the belated hope of lulling Clem's suspicion but knowing only too well he was not as guileless as that. She ought to have followed Midge's example and just shrugged. Why did one always think of the better thing to say when it was too late?

She would have been puzzled as well as surprised by the look that followed her. Clem's face had matched his hair at her taunt but now the color faded and he watched the slim figure cross the field, head high, with a slow smile of approval. Convinced that she had not only seen Jarret on the train but might even know his destination, Clem could not help admiring her for not giving the boy away.

CHAPTER V

At Trois Lacs

"Oh, Clem! I thought you'd be here this afternoon."

Claire sounded disappointed and Denis wondered why. Since she was helping Midge pick burrs out of Charcoal's long, silky ears on the back gallery, she could not help overhear the conversation in the hall. Before Clem went in he had casually asked if she and Midge would care to drive to Trois Lacs with him after lunch. A peace offering? In any case, her desire to see Jarret's original destination was stronger than the wish to snub Clem. Although she had not leaped at the suggestion as Midge did, she had accepted.

"Must you go to Trois Lacs?" Claire repeated.

"Yes, Dad needs some things. Why this sudden yen for my company?"

"Only that I told—— I mean it's such a nice day for tennis. Bruce Walker wants to come out and I thought we could play doubles."

"You mean that cousin of the Thompsons? Works for the textile people? Good looking? Too good looking, if you ask me," Clem grunted.

"You're just envious, Red."

"Envious, my foot! Am I envious of Tubby?"

"Tubby!" Claire was scornful.

"Anyway, if handsome-and-knows-it is coming out he wants to see you, my beautiful sister. Play singles with him if he must have his tennis."

"I thought it might be pleasant for Dee, too," said Claire.

"Well, Dee doesn't have to go to Trois Lacs. Midge and I will go alone."

It was then Denis heard her aunt's voice. Midge could go nowhere that afternoon out of sight of the house. She would learn to leave frogs outside perhaps. As always Aunt Felice spoke quickly and with decision. Denise must go, however, because she wanted some things a boy would not know how to buy.

So Denis drove off with Clem soon after lunch, taking explicit verbal instructions as well as a list of purchases carefully written in both French and English. When they started toward the mountains she pointed toward the southwest and said in surprise, "I thought Trois Lacs was that way."

"Good thing you aren't a bird," said Clem. "You'd be flying north in winter and south for the summer. That way would take you to La Baie and Côte L'Avenir—eventually."

He was driving her a long way around it was true, Clem admitted, because he wanted to stop at the Dulac place and see Jeanpierre's uncle who was there for a few days. But it was the prettiest route even if the mountain road was not too good; and she would see a hill parish that would give her a real idea of French Canada.

From the crest of the first hill Denis looked back at the old manor house and asked a question that had been bothering her. How, when almost everyone around was French, did the Frasers happen to own *Manoir Laurent?*

Clem explained that *Manoir Laurent*, all that remained of the original seigneury of that name, had come to the Frasers when her great-grandmother, a Laurent, married a Scot of that name. The property went to her son of course, Denis Laurent Fraser. In French Canada it was not uncommon for property to remain two hundred and fifty years in the same family or some branch of it.

"Grandfather carried on the name Laurent by giving it to his eldest son," Clem added. "As a pianist Grandfather prefers to be known as Denis Laurent."

"You mean that is Uncle Guy's middle name?"

"Yes. Why don't you ask where I come in?"

But Denis was not to be lured into another squabble. She said nothing.

"I wasn't selected for the red hair, you know."

Clem gave his attention to a bad stretch of road before he explained briefly that his father had been a close friend of her uncle's. Robert Clement, Guy and Duncan Fraser had bought the asbestos mine property together. Guy was too busy running the farm at *Manoir Laurent* to take an active part but Clem's father had helped start the mine. But then Duncan Fraser had bought them both out.

"My mother died when I was born and father lived only a few years after that. When he died your uncle adopted me."

"And changed your name to Clement Fraser."

"Yes, he wanted me to feel that I was truly his son and I couldn't ask for a better father. When Uncle Duncan proposed that I work in the mine my own father helped to start, Dad said I could do as I liked."

"So you went to an agricultural college."

"Right." The way Clem said it betrayed his satisfaction.

"Dad wants to make *Manoir Laurent* a modern, outstanding farm and I want to help. Dad's tops."

Denis could agree on that. Uncle Guy was tops with her, too. But beneath Clem's tribute she sensed something close to worship of the older man. They were in the hills now and a thick growth of spruce, fir and tamarack crowded the road on either side. Clem pointed out a trail on the right. It led to Birch Lake which was the shortest way to Salmon Creek where he liked to fish.

"Take you along someday," he offered, adding that the lake was on their own property as was much of the stream. "Dulac's place used to be part of the Laurent seigneury, too. But he owns it now. Here we are."

Clem stopped his car before the house at the turn of the road and got out, leaving Denis to think about what he had told her. He was the first boy she had known who wanted to be a farmer and she had a feeling that it was not only because of his devotion to Uncle Guy. He seemed to have the same love of the land that the habitants had.

She glanced curiously at the small habitant house around which Clem had disappeared. It was set close to the road and the bright blue trim around windows and door, the steeply pitched roof, were typical. There was the usual narrow gallery along the front, barely wide enough for the rocker in which an old woman sat knitting. It was an old man, however, who seemed to be in charge of the fat baby.

Presently someone came around the corner of the house, singing. It was Jeanpierre. In his plaid wool shirt, with red socks rolled over his high boots, he belonged in the picture. He touched his cap politely when he saw Denis, said something in French to the old people and then walked off down the road over which they had come, still singing lustily.

"Ki-ti-ke-ti-ke-tac."

Denis hummed the tune while his voice grew fainter and fainter until it faded into the distance.

"See Jeanpierre?" said Clem when he finally came out and

found her still humming. "He's off to Laurentville for his Saturday fun."

"The movies?"

Clem nodded. "And maybe a 'Sing' later. Or a dance. Wait until you see Jeanpierre on skates. He taught both Jarret and me. And he's almost as good on skis."

The road was narrow and poor. In spite of Clem's skill, they bumped over ruts and into unseen holes as they continued to climb. When he had to shift into low gear, Clem remarked that they were climbing the last hill. After that it would be downgrade all the way to Trois Lacs.

"There's a good view at the top of this one," he promised. "Better in winter of course. Then you can sometimes catch a glimpse of Hidden Pond."

"Hidden Pond?" Denis repeated. "Not really hidden?"

Clem explained that Hidden Pond was actually a small lake surrounded by hills and with no approach from any road. Back in the early days, when Canada was a French possession, the property belonged to an associate of the unscrupulous Intendant, Bigot. Now it was owned by a disagreeable old habitant and few people had even seen the Pond. Thus the name.

"Jarret and I discovered a connection with Birch Lake and we used to fish the Pond occasionally until old Jules caught us. This summer he put up barbed wire and we couldn't get in."

Clem shut off his motor at the top of the hill and showed her a break in the trees where *Manoir Laurent* could be seen far below. And that small patch of water in the left foreground was the south end of Birch Lake. The Pond was this side of the lake, completely hidden by the heavily wooded hills.

"Even in winter you can only catch a glimpse of it," said Clem as they got back into the car. "The Pond's well named, even without the old legend."

"Another legend?" said Denis.

"So you've heard a few? Well garnished, I'll warrant, if

Angelica told them." Yes, French Canada had its legends, Clem admitted. There were several versions of this one.

In the time of the unscrupulous Bigot, so the story ran, the *château* that included Hidden Pond was the summer residence of a mysterious man close to the Intendant—some said it was Bigot himself. In any event, according to the story, the owner, while hunting in the woods, met and fell in love with a beautiful Indian maiden. He took her back to his *château* and secreted her in the tower on Hidden Pond. Sometime later, on his return from a visit to the palace in Quebec, he found her dead in the tower. And no one could tell what had happened.

"It is said that she was discovered by her Indian father and killed by him when she refused to return to the woods. So the legend runs," said Clem and added skeptically that much the same tale was told of a ruined manor house nearer Quebec.

"Does the habitant who now owns the place live in the old *château?*" Denis asked.

"No, that burned down long ago. Only the stone tower on Hidden Pond remains."

"Have you been in it?"

Clem shook his head. "There's no door. And the entrance to any passage from the *château* has long since been buried in the ruins. When we were kids Jarret and I tried more than once to find the passage but we never could."

But how exciting, thought Denis, as they started down the hill. Only Clem could be so prosaic about it. Imagine a mysterious tower without an entrance, a tower with a romantic history! On a hidden pond! And practically next door to *Manoir Laurent!* Could she see it? She must.

The road flattened out at the foot of the hill and the forest receded, giving room for a small settlement. This was the hill parish of Côte de Montagne, Clem explained, as he stopped the car.

"In winter it looks exactly like a painting by Gagnon or Caron," he said, indicating the modest houses, with their brightly colored trim, grouped about a church. The men who lived here worked in the lumber camps when winter came, Clem confided, and it had occurred to him that Jarret might have some such idea.

"Not that I want to give him away to Uncle Duncan. Only —well, he's pretty young. I'd like to find out where he is just in case——" Clem broke off, then demanded unexpectedly, "Any notion, Dee?"

Denis was not prepared for the question. "Why—should I have?" she stammered in confusion and was thankful when Clem merely shrugged and got out of the car without following up his advantage.

Disturbed, she watched him speak to one of the men near the church and then go into the house of another. Was Jarret bound for the lumber camps? Was that why his destination had been Trois Lacs. Perhaps, under the circumstances, she ought to tell Clem about the ticket receipt tucked away in her purse.

While she pondered, a group of children had gathered about the car, eyeing it and her at first shyly and then with bold curiosity. By the time Clem came back, one of them was standing on the running board in order to peer inside and report in his special brand of French to the others.

"Gurr! That child! Garlic!" Denis shuddered, holding her nose as they started off.

Clem laughed at her. "What's wrong with garlic? You eat it in Ma Tante's salad."

"But that boy was steeped in it; the girl too. And they all stared at me. Because of Grandfather, I suppose."

Clem gave her a skeptical glance. She must know she was easy to look at. Could a girl so conscious of her possible importance be unaware she was pretty? He decided that she was, or at least not thinking about it, and chalked up a mark to her credit.

One of the habitants waved as they passed. He had swung a young child to his shoulder and was singing to it.

Denis covered her ears. "He's off key."

"Is he?" said Clem.

"Badly." To prove it she mimicked the voice of the habitant in an impromptu jargon.

"Aren't you overcritical?"

"Of course not. I'd say better not sing if you cannot do better than that."

"And I'd say better sing off key than not at all."

"What non——" Denis was jounced out of her seat as they went into a hole and came out with a jolt. "—sense!" she finished and added crossly, "Isn't it smoother on the other side of the road?"

"If it were, I'd drive there," Clem informed her.

Denis gave him an indignant glance and subsided into outraged silence. Why should he be so disagreeable just because she had said that habitant couldn't sing? Now she could not ask whether he had learned anything about Jarret. Even when they went into another hole and she hit the top of the car she did not make a sound.

"Sorry," Clem said gruffly.

Around the next bend the town of Trois Lacs came into view. But there was a baker's cart just ahead, buff color with *Boulanger* painted in red on the sides. The driver sat far back so that all she could see of him were his hands on the reins as he pulled his horse over to let them pass. The road was so narrow Clem had to creep by in order to keep out of the ditch and he did not speak again until he stopped under a tree on the main street of the town and shut off his motor.

"Gosh!" he said then. "This Jarret business bothers me."

"You did not learn anything?" When Clem shook his head Denis started to speak, checked herself and instead of telling him about the ticket receipt announced suddenly, "I believe Midge knows or suspects what Jarret is up to."

"So do I," Clem agreed. "The trouble is that if Midge doesn't choose to talk you might as well try to get information from the Sphinx. Only Grandfather could do it. I wish he were here."

"Midge is a lamb," Denis murmured affectionately.

"That is something on which we *can* agree," Clem declared emphatically. "But come along, we may as well get the shopping done."

Denis was not impressed by Trois Lacs. Its sole claim to distinction seemed to be the fact that it was the birthplace of one of Canada's foremost political leaders. The town boasted a variety of stores, however, all unprepossessing, and was obviously a shopping centre for the surrounding villages. Horse-drawn vehicles as well as cars and bicycles were parked the length of the main street.

But what could Trois Lacs offer Jarret? To Denis it seemed but a dull town, making a ludicrous attempt to go modern. She laughed over the modest restaurant that was signed a dignified "Chez Gerard" in French but in English "Quick Lunch".

"That's for the benefit of the tourists from the States," said Clem.

He left her at the store where she was to purchase cheese-cloth and thread and towelling and the rest. She found it overcrowded with poorly arranged merchandise. Men's shirts and slickers were laid out beside baby socks and piece goods; heavy boots crowded net curtains. There were candies and tobacco and notepaper as well as dresses and linoleum and hats. The Frenchman who ran the store could speak little English, his wife none, and Denis soon discovered that, as Aunt Felice had feared, she would need the French list.

The last article had been purchased and checked off and the things were being wrapped when a habitant came in. Denis, who was buying candies for Midge from the woman, would not have noticed the newcomer had he not stared at her. That drew her attention and she glanced surreptitiously in his direction when he began to talk to the storekeeper.

The latter had paused in the wrapping of her packages to examine what the habitant showed him, something that looked like a piece of greenish grey stone with shreds of white cotton sticking to it. They discussed it in their patois with garrulous interest until finally the storekeeper returned to his wrapping and the habitant turned away. Whereupon a startled exclamation escaped Denis.

"Bon jour, mademoiselle." He doffed his cap, slid the stone into his pocket and swaggered out.

Denis stared after him in dismay. His necktie! That he had worn one at all was singular enough for a habitant. But it was the necktie Jarret had worn on the train; she knew it was! She could not possibly be mistaken because the spot was still on it, the spot that looked like a beetle.

Back in the car, she waited for Clem and wondered how to tell him she had seen a man wearing Jarret's necktie without admitting she had seen Jarret on the train. She ought to have asked the name of the man because she would find it hard to describe him. All she could say was that he was dark, and that oddly enough his hands were familiar to her; somewhere she had seen them before. Would Clem know who he was if she said the man had big, squarish brown hands with stubby fingers? On the way home she approached the subject in a roundabout fashion.

"I wish I could understand these habitants," Denis complained. "In the store it was exasperating not to be able to understand what they jabbered at me."

Clem laughed. "It's easy enough to pick up their patois if you know French."

"I don't," said Denis. "As you are very well aware. Oh, just a little."

"Then why not learn?" Clem challenged, pointing out that both her aunt and Claire spoke perfect French. "I'll suggest we speak it at meals," he told her with a provocative grin. "If you have to ask for your food in French or go hungry, you'll soon learn a lot."

Denis only nodded peaceably. She wanted to get back to the habitant with Jarret's necktie and was about to broach the subject from a different angle when Clem tipped his head in the direction of the back seat.

"By the by, that fishing rod is for you."

"Fishing rod! But I don't fish."

"You soon will. I promised Midge I'd take her up to Birch Lake next week and you can come along," Clem offered carelessly.

"Thank you," said Denis with frigid dignity. "But Miss Fraser regrets."

"Going to be busy at the piano, eh?"

Denis bit back a furious retort. She would not be goaded into another bicker over her music; it was too important. And why had she ever entertained the notion of telling this creature about Jarret's ticket. She would say nothing. She wouldn't even speak, since anything she said led to a fight and she was not going to squabble with anyone so—so insignificant.

They rode in silence for three or four miles and then Clem began to sing. It was Jeanpierre's song of earlier in the afternoon and the rhythm was impelling.

> Que le moulin marchait
> Et dans son joli chant disait
> Ke-ti-ke-ti-ke-tac
> Ke-ti-ke-ti-ke-tac.

"It means," Clem explained amiably as though nothing had happened, "the mill ran on its way and in its pretty song would sing Ketiketiketac. Come on, try it in French."

And somehow, in spite of her determination to put Clem in his place, Denis was singing with him when they turned into the *Manoir Laurent* road half an hour later. Nothing more had been said about Jarret or the habitant with the yellow tie and she had come to the conclusion that, regardless of the beetle spot, it probably was not Jarret's tie at all but only one like it.

CHAPTER VI

In Green Pencil

DENIS WAS GLAD she had taken Claire's advice and brought two sweaters because out of the sun it was cold, especially on this path through the woods. How she happened to be headed for a day of fishing with Clem and Midge was hard to say, except that Clem had an exasperating habit of getting what he wanted and he was determined she should learn to fish. The fields had been covered with a glistening layer of frost earlier that morning and now it was the sort of crisp October day that made one feel happily alive, eager to be in the open. Perhaps that was why, despite her resolve not to come, here she was.

It was some time since Clem had bought her the fishpole at Trois Lacs. She had been at *Manoir Laurent* over a month but until today he had been too busy to go fishing and, indeed, she had seen little of him except at meals or when the others were there. That was one reason why she had said nothing about the man with the yellow tie.

The lunch basket was getting heavy and Denis put it down in order to rest. Clem, ahead with the poles and blanket and paddles, was out of sight and Midge lagged in the rear. A rustle in the dry leaves followed by the chatter of a squirrel broke the quiet of the woods and then Denis was aware of another sound that came faintly, from far off, the very ghost of a sound. Was it music? Or was it the wind singing through the tops of the firs high above her head?

She stood very still, her head tipped back to listen, but all she heard now was a familiar sound from Midge who always gave little chirps or coos of delight when she found anything that pleased her.

"Oooh! Oooh!"

"What is it?" called Denis.

"A caterpillar, a big, furry one. He's yellow! I'll bring him."

Denis picked up the lunch basket with a smile of relief. While a caterpillar was not her idea of a pleasant addition to their party, he might so easily have been a snake. She walked on, preoccupied with the more important problem of Jarret and guiltily aware that she ought to have told Clem long ago about the man at Trois Lacs.

One thing after another had kept her from doing so. Even before they reached home that afternoon she had decided that if harm had come to Jarret the habitant would scarcely have worn his tie. And Clem would be sure to rag her about the beetle spot. How could anyone say a spot was the same? She was loath to give Jarret away, even to Clem, and the more she thought about it the less likely it seemed that the yellow tie was his. The message in green pencil made her wish she had talked to Clem.

It was because Uncle Duncan was in New York on business that the mine superintendent had sent the message in green pencil on to Uncle Guy. Printed on an ordinary post card, in an obvious attempt to conceal the writer's identity, the thing had arrived this morning while they were having breakfast.

YOUR SON JARRET SEEN
NEAR COURCEVILLE.
LOOKED WELL AND HAPPY.

Could Jarret himself have written it? Uncle Guy and Clem did not think so. They said Jarret was too honest; if ready to go home he would go and if not he wouldn't mislead his father as to his whereabouts. What did it mean then? Uncle

Guy went off without finishing his breakfast to make some inquiries and Aunt Felice frowned over the post card.

And then something else had happened. When the lunch basket was ready Denis took it out to the car and passed Aunt Felice who was just turning away from the butcher's cart. As the butcher gathered up the reins, only his hands visible, Denis stopped short with an involuntary exclamation.

"Have you forgotten something?" said Aunt Felice.

"No, I've just—remembered something."

To avoid further questions Denis hurried on with the lunch. Now she knew where she had seen the hands of the Frenchman who wore Jarret's tie. They belonged to the driver of a cart like the one driving off, the baker's cart she and Clem had passed on the road from Côte de Montagne to Trois Lacs. But how had a baker of Trois Lacs come by Jarret's tie if Jarret was somewhere in the vicinity of Courceville?

That was what she must talk to Clem about, Denis decided, as she picked up the lunch basket and followed him to the lake. By the time she got there Clem had the canoe in the water. He explained that since Dulac was overhauling the big boat this week they would have to fish from the rocks south of Salmon Creek and use the canoe to cross the lake.

"We picked a good day, eh?"

"Perfect," Denis agreed. *"Un beau jour!"*

It was warm in the sun by the water and the lake was blue below the white trunks of the birches that fringed it. Most of the birches had already lost their yellow leaves but an occasional maple flamed red against the dark green of the spruce and fir.

Clem took a moment to inspect the caterpillar Midge had brought on a leaf. "Yes, he's a beauty. But hop up in the bow so we can get started. Dee's going to sit in the middle."

As he pushed off and began to paddle across the lake, Denis said again, *"Un beau jour!"*

Clem laughed. "Don't you get enough French at meals? How is it coming, by the way?"

"Well enough, I suppose. When you all chatter at once I'm lost but I can understand Claire and some of what Jeanpierre says now. He speaks very slowly to me."

"That's like him. Jeanpierre is good, always patient, always kind. And the farm means as much to him as it does to Dad and me. I believe he loves every handful of dirt on the place."

"Claire says I'm getting along all right with the French," Denis admitted, but looked so dubious that Clem grinned.

"I notice food is your specialty."

"But I'm so hungry all the time. I'm hungry right now."

Clem laughed again and said she was as bad as Angie. The lunch basket looked adequate, however, even for her. In addition they would have fish.

"Suppose we don't catch any?"

"But we will, Dee," Midge asserted confidently. "Jarret says Birch Lake ought to be called Salmon Heaven."

Jarret! Denis looked thoughtfully at Clem as he dipped his paddle in and out with long, even strokes, before she asked in a low tone, "Do you think Jarret is somewhere around Courceville as the card said?"

64

Clem frowned and shook his head. "I think it is most unlikely."

"Then how do you account for the message in green pencil? Aunt Felice, especially, seemed so upset by it."

Clem shrugged. "Courceville is a small village with one store and a Franciscan Seminary on the river."

A seminary! Could that be where—— She looked at Clem and knew that he had guessed her thought. But a slight inclination of his head warned her that Midge could hear and Denis said nothing more. Yet somehow she must manage to tell Clem today about the man at Trois Lacs.

On the far side of the lake Clem headed for a shallow patch of sand near the mouth of Salmon Creek, beached the canoe and parked the lunch basket in the shade. They would fish from the great rocks that bordered the lake beyond the creek, where the water was deep and cold, a haven for salmon.

The air was now so much warmer that Denis left her extra sweater behind when they started up the brook to a place where there were easy steppingstones across. A few minutes later she was established on top of a great boulder, a fishpole in her hands, a suitable fly on the end of her line and instructions to play the fish if she got a bite.

Clem and Midge picked their way along the rocks to other boulders, and the rocky shore beyond Denis curved inward, making it possible for her to see them when each finally selected a perch. She did not really want to fish. She would rather just sit in the sun and watch the others. Across the rocky cove she saw Midge catch the first salmon and watched the skillful way Clem cast for another. He landed one and cast again while her own fly floated unheeded on the surface of the water. Suddenly it disappeared, the pole jerked and the reel began to click as the line played out. A bite!

"I have a bite," Denis cried. "A bite!" Frantically she reeled in the line while the salmon fought and the pole bent to his struggle. Oooh! She could see him now. He was tremendous.

Clem shouted a warning but she was too excited to hear. As the fish neared the surface she let go of the reel in order to grab the pole with both hands and lift him out, leaning back to give a mighty heave. But then something happened; the weight was suddenly gone, the pole ceased to bend, Mr. Salmon was off the hook. The pole slid into the water as

Denis pawed the air in an effort to keep her balance, failed and toppled in after it.

Somehow she managed to swim ashore and cling to the rocks, although the water was like ice and her teeth had begun to chatter before Clem arrived and helped her climb out.

"Now I kn—ow why f—fish are co—old blooded."

Clem surveyed her in dismay—the dripping strings of hair, sodden blue jeans and soggy mass of sweater. "Fine mermaid!" he groaned and said there was only one thing to do. She must go back to the sandy place where they had beached the canoe, remove her clothes and wrap herself in the blanket until they dried.

"Good thing the sun is strong. Why the dickens didn't you play that fish as I told you to?" he grumbled.

"Did you s—see him? Wasn't he a wh-whopper?" Denis chattered.

But Clem was in no mood to talk of a fish that got away. He hurried her around to the sunny beach and left her, with orders to get out of the wet clothes and fast.

"I'll be back inside of five minutes to start a fire and make some coffee. So make it snappy," he ordered.

Again Denis was thankful for the extra sweater. It could be worn as a blouse while the blanket became a kind of sarong, and thus clad she felt none the worse for her cold dip. She spread out the lunch and ate a piece of bread and butter while she watched Clem clean and fry the fish.

"Uhm! The coffee smells good and I'm so hungry."

"You're always hungry," said Clem. "Didn't they feed you in the States?"

Even that irritating expression, the States, failed to provoke Denis today. She bit into another slice of homemade bread spread with sweet butter and laughed, "Not like this. Besides, I'm not used to icewater dips. I could eat all the fish," she told him shamelessly.

"You don't deserve even a piece," Clem grunted.

But he gave her the major share along with a lecture on

how to handle a reel and other instructions that she could not put to test because her blue jeans were as yet far from dry. And she couldn't very well fish in a blanket.

Midge giggled softly at the idea and Clem said what she really needed was a form of diving suit. Since that was not available she would have to stay here in the sun while he and Midge fished. If her clothes were dry when they got back he might show her Hidden Pond.

Denis, who was eating another apple tart with her second cup of coffee and feeling lazily content, looked about the lake with fresh interest. "Where is Hidden Pond from here?" she asked eagerly.

Clem had started to clean the frying pan. He said the pond was north of them of course. "I told you that the day we drove to Trois Lacs," he reminded her.

"Yes," Denis said meekly. Always confused by points of the compass, she looked around the lake again and wondered which was the north side but decided not to invite any caustic remarks by asking. It did not matter. What mattered was seeing this Hidden Pond with its romantic tower.

After Clem and Midge went off to fish again, Denis packed away the remains of the lunch and then, stretched prone on the sand, thought about the tower without a door. Had the mysterious Indian girl really died there? Or was the story only, as Clem had suggested, one of the more popular legends of French Canada?

The water of the lake lapped the shore gently, an intermittent wind stirred the few remaining leaves on the birches and at intervals a bird flew in or out of the woods. A sense of deep contentment possessed Denis. She had already begun to understand what Clem meant when he asserted that people who didn't live on a farm did not live, they just existed.

At *Manoir Laurent* every day was full; there were apples to pick now, nuts to gather, young calves and pigs to watch and each day brought some fresh excitement. Her house chores finished, Denis was as eager as Charcoal or Nicolette to be out-of-doors and she never had felt so alive. Yes, she had begun to see why Clem felt the way he did about the farm and even to understand why he liked to hunt and fish. She would rather like to go back and have another try for that salmon herself, except that her clothes were not dry and it was so pretty here by the lake.

It was peaceful without being lonely. There were live things all about, small furry animals and even deer in the surrounding woods. Denis had not lived in the same house with Midge for the past several weeks without learning that. Yes, she was sorry for people who lived in cities and towns, thought Denis, and cradled her head on crossed arms contentedly.

She awoke suddenly sometime later, blinked against the sun, then hastily rolled over and sat up. Thank goodness! The yellow caterpillar who had been asking her to dance with him was only a dream. Ugh! She had shuddered away from the creature who stood at least six feet tall as he bowed ceremoniously before her and wriggled his tractor-like feet to the music.

Yet even in her dream it had seemed a pity he was not human, because the music was so gay. She could almost remember its rhythmic melody. Denis began to hum, then stopped abruptly and tipped her head to catch what sounded like the very strain of music she had dreamed. Or was she still dreaming? She jumped up, listening for the sound that had seemed to come from the hilly shore to her left. But she could no longer hear it. Had she ever done so?

Denis gave herself a shake. What a silly dream!

The wind had risen while she slept and was whipping the lake into small waves, blowing her hair about wildly. Her clothes, spread over the canoe to dry, were no longer there. She found some on the beach, her blouse and bras swung from the limb of a birch and her jeans flapped in protest against the bush on which they were caught. Happily the wind that scattered had also dried all but the sweater so that when she had managed, with the help of a canoe paddle to recover the blouse, Denis retired behind a bush and hastily exchanged the blanket for her own garments.

Back in the sun, she ran a pocket comb through her hair and hummed to herself until she heard Clem and Midge coming when she broke off with a faint snicker. Suppose she told them she had dreamed Midge's yellow caterpillar asked her to dance and that she was trying to recall the tune?

Midge would probably feel she ought not to have turned the creature down, thought Denis. But Clem would say she had eaten too much lunch.

"What did you do?" he demanded when she had inspected his catch and Midge's. "Sleep?"

"Part of the time," said Denis and asked quickly, "Clem, where did you say Hidden Pond was from here?"

Clem groaned. "Gosh, you'd better not get lost in the woods, Dee. I said it was due north, over there, the other side of the hill."

When he pointed in the direction from which she thought she had heard the faint sound of music, Denis started and then unaccountably shivered.

"Have you caught cold?" Clem demanded sharply.

Anyway, they had better start for home, he decided. She could see the Pond some other time. The sun was already off the west side of the lake and the wind blowing up colder. On a day like this the temperature could drop ten degrees in as many minutes. Even a sudden snowstorm was possible.

"In October?" Denis said skeptically.

"Yes, in October. Here, wrap yourself in the blanket and don't argue."

"But I'm not catching cold," Denis objected. "I just—shivered."

Unfortunately she shivered again whereupon Clem flung the blanket at her. "Get in," he ordered, his face a match for the red hair that the wind was now blowing straight up in a comical fashion.

Denis eyed his head and pretended to shrink back timidly.

"Are you quite sure the sparks won't start a fire on the way over?"

Clem glared down at her, then recovered his temper as suddenly as he had lost it. "Put the blanket around you and get into the canoe, Dee," he said quietly.

Something warned Denis to obey but she waved aside his offer of help, and head high, stepped into the canoe, only to trip over the blanket. If Clem had not reached out a long arm and grasped hers, she would have pitched headlong into the water on the other side. Instead, she collapsed without ceremony into the bottom of the boat, untangled herself and looked up haughtily. Clem was laughing at her, of course.

No, his long chin thrust out doggedly, he prepared to push off, his grim expression an absurd contrast to the blowzy red hair. Denis snickered, choked and finally doubled up with mirth.

"What's so funny?" Clem demanded.

"Me. And—you. And me," Denis managed.

Clem's surprised look became a grin of approval that was like a pat on the head and then suddenly he was laughing with her.

"You're rocking the canoe," Midge objected.

"So we are. And not getting anywhere." Clem dipped his paddle into the water again.

Away from the shore the wind was cold and they made slow headway against the choppy little waves. Denis was soon thankful for the blanket and said so, privately giving Clem a credit when he did not crow but said maybe they would get back for another picnic before the lake froze.

"If not, you can skate through the channel for a look at Hidden Pond."

Not that there was much to see, he told her. Just the old tower and she could only view that from a distance because of the barbed wire.

"The Pond was a great place to skate until old Jules shut us out," Clem grumbled.

Denis wondered what he would say if she told him she had

heard music from that direction; probably that she had imagined it. But real or a dream, she could not seem to get the tantalizing strain out of her head, although she could not quite recapture it either. All the way home the memory of it plagued her until she began to wish she had been less emphatic about touching the piano. By the time Clem dropped her off at the house Denis had decided that somehow she must pin down that haunting melody.

If Claire was not around she might try it on the piano right now. She had seen Aunt Felice out feeding her beloved geese, Midge and Clem would be cleaning fish in the barn and Uncle Guy was seldom in the house at this time of day. If only Claire was——

Denis actually jumped, for just as she reached the door it opened and there was Claire herself. And obviously something was wrong.

"What has happened? Is it—Jarret?" Denis gasped, for that was her first guilty thought. Oh, why had she not managed to tell Clem what she knew?

But Claire shook her head, glanced cautiously toward the stairway and said in a low tone, "No, but I thought I had better tell you. Angelica is here. She—— It was Angie who wrote the message in green pencil."

CHAPTER VII

Something for Clem

ANGELICA HAD BEEN confined to her room for three days, even for meals, while Aunt Felice went about solemnly determined, Uncle Guy troubled, and Midge who hated anything to be shut up, unhappy. Claire thought it was the hardest punishment her sister could have had for sending the message in green pencil.

"It was too bad of Angie," said Claire. "But after all, no harm was done because Uncle Duncan was not there to see the card and get upset over it.

"That," Clem pointed out, "is probably what Angie minds most."

Of course, if the mine superintendent had merely read the card over the telephone instead of mailing it on to Uncle Guy, they might never have known who sent it. Unfortunately, when Aunt Felice saw it, some of the print looked all too familiar. The writer had Angelica's habit of mixing upper and lower case printed letters. When her mother remembered that Angelica had spent the week end with a school friend a few miles from Courceville, she hunted out some old valentines. On those sent to her by Angie the capital L in "Love" proved a perfect match for that in the "Looked" of the green pencil message.

Ordered home from school and confronted with the card, Angelica readily admitted writing it. Why? Because it was silly of Uncle Duncan to make such a fuss about finding Jarret, who would not have run away if he wanted to be found. Why couldn't they leave him alone? Nothing could have happened to him; dead people were always discovered.

Since Aunt Felice and Uncle Guy did not share this point

of view, Angelica had spent three days in her room, a punishment she took philosophically.

"I just wanted to make it easier for Jarret," Denis overheard her tell Clem.

"You mean harder for Uncle Duncan," Clem corrected.

Angelica shrugged.

This morning she would return to school by train and had appeared at the breakfast table with less than usual to say but otherwise seemingly unperturbed. Uncle Guy was not there, having left for Montreal the night before, and Claire had gone for an early horseback ride with Bruce Walker.

"How can she ride without breakfast?" exclaimed Angelica. "Is he that attractive?"

"So it seems," Clem said sourly.

Angelica gave him a keen glance before she helped herself to a final sausage and one more pancake. "Well, I just hope he has as good taste in sweets as Tubby. We haven't had a French chocolate around here since Claire quarreled with Tubby."

"Don't you think of anything but food?" Clem demanded.

"You'd think about it yourself if you had to swallow the flavorless fodder they serve us at school."

"Cheer up! What you've just consumed ought to last the first forty-eight hours," said Clem. But his grin was not unsympathetic.

Angelica looked chastened after she had said good-by to her mother and was ready to leave for the train. To Denis she seemed younger than usual in her school coat and with books under her arm. While they waited outside for Clem to get the bag, Claire rode into the yard with Bruce Walker, who saluted Denis and smiled gallantly down at Angie when Claire introduced him.

"So this is the little sister. Ah, to be young! And off to boarding school."

"*Mais oui!* A happy age," said Angie demurely. "Perhaps you would like to take my place. I'm sure the little girls

74

would welcome the substitution," she added, her black eyes a mischievous challenge.

"Good for Angie," muttered Clem who had just come out with the suitcase.

As Angelica got into the car Bruce Walker's interested gaze followed her and Denis was conscious of a sudden distaste for Claire's new beau. Instinctively she looked at his hands on the reins and her dislike increased. They were too small, too narrow and—and sleek.

Clem started his motor and shot off down the road with Angie. Claire rode on to the barn and Bruce Walker jogged off toward Laurentville, leaving Denis to wonder why Claire liked him. He was so old for one thing, Why, he must be thirty. She watched him put his horse to a trot, unaware that a few feet away Jeanpierre was also watching.

She started when the French boy spoke and offered her a clumsy sort of bundle, saying that his uncle had sent it. Would she please see that M'sieu Clem got the package as soon as he returned?

Of course she would. Denis took the bundle which was poorly wrapped in newspaper and tied clumsily with frayed twine.

"Oh, Jeanpierre," she called as the French boy started for the barn. "Aunt Felice wants some wood brought in. *Quelque bois à bruler.*"

Rather proud of her growing ability to make Jeanpierre understand, Denis went into the house with the bundle, wondering because of its softness, what the contents could be. She had volunteered to do all the downstairs dusting this morning because Aunt Felice and Curly Rose wanted to make apple jelly. Moreover, with Claire baking bread and Midge at school, this would be her opportunity to use the piano and try to pick out that tantalizing melody she had heard, or dreamed, the day they went fishing.

Denis put the bundle for Clem on a chair near the door and was busily at work with her duster when Jeanpierre brought in the first armful of wood. Mr. Chip, who was now a gen-

eral pet and had the run of the house, moved with her from
chair to table, table to chest. The lame chipmunk's friendly
desire for company was second only to his curiosity. Even
Angelica admitted that he was an engaging "rat" and he had
soon made friends with the dogs who enjoyed chasing him
about but would settle down for a snooze with Mr. Chip between them. He had but one enemy, Muff.

There had always been a kind of cold war between Muff
and the dogs. The cat ignored Charcoal and Nicolette and
they were wise enough to avoid active engagements, but
neither had any love of the big Persian. Mr. Chip shared their
dislike but, unlike the dogs, he was afraid. For Muff, old, fat
and no match in speed for the Chipmunk even though he
was lame, managed to convey the impression that she was
only waiting; her time would come and when it did she would
make short work of him.

Meanwhile, if Muff stalked into the room, tail straight up
and waving gently at the tip, the chipmunk would scamper up
a drapery or somewhere out of reach and chatter down at her
impudently. But his very chatter always betrayed his fear.

Mr. Chip was investigating the string on Clem's bundle,
while Denis dusted a nearby table, when Jeanpierre came in
with some wood. Not only Charcoal but Muff had slid into
the house with him and although the big cat padded silently
into the living room, Mr. Chip knew instantly that she was
there. He leaped to the safety of Denis's shoulder and chattered nervously at his enemy.

Muff paused, her tail waved faster, then, without turning
her head, she stalked majestically to a spot of sun by the east
window, sat down and commenced an unhurried toilet.

Charcoal, on the other hand, barked an invitation to romp
which the chipmunk had started to accept when he thought
better of it and scurried back to his safe perch. Evidently he
considered that the Cocker alone was insufficient protection
against the enemy.

Denis glanced at Muff washing her face with such aloof
grace. "I think you would be safer and happier up in my

room this morning, Mr. Chip," she decided and ran upstairs with him.

Back in the living room, she found Charcoal playing with a loose end of the twine that tied Clem's bundle. He had the string in his mouth and was already backing up with it.

"Charcoal!"

But it was too late. The frayed twine broke and the bundle opened, spreading its contents over the floor. Denis gasped and stared down at them while Charcoal made off with his share of the twine. Denis was so startled and alarmed by the contents of the bundle that it was a full minute before she discovered that Jeanpierre was looking at them, too.

Hastily she knelt and tried to gather the tweed suit and brown shirt into their paper wrapping, her one thought being to get them out of sight until Clem came back. They were the clothes Jarret had worn that day on the train when he told her he was running away. And he had had no bag, nothing that might contain another suit of clothes. She felt suddenly a little sick and terribly frightened.

"Where—where did your uncle get these?" she demanded of Jeanpierre.

The French boy looked blank and· shook his head. He did not know; his uncle had said only that the *paquet* was for Clem.

Denis had waved aside his offer of help but as she scrambled the clothes together in the paper, something hard rolled out and Jeanpierre quickly stooped and picked it up. There was a peculiar expression on his face as, reluctantly Denis thought, he handed her a sizable pocket knife. She dropped the knife into a pocket of the tweed coat, to which was pinned a note addressed to Clem, tied the awkward bundle with what remained of the twine and put it away in the hall closet as Jeanpierre went off to get more wood.

The door had scarcely closed behind him when she heard the car and saw Clem drive past the kitchen wing on his way to the barn. Denis snatched a sweater from the hall closet and flew out after him. Yesterday she had told Clem about the man in Trois Lacs. He knew now that she had seen Jarret on the train and seen him get off at La Baie after he told her he was running away. The only thing she had not mentioned was the ticket to Trois Lacs that was still tucked away in the zipper pocket of her purse. Now, breathlessly, she told him about the bundle.

A few minutes later they opened it together in Uncle Guy's little office between the hall and dining room and Clem scowled apprehensively at the contents before he read the note from Jean Dulac. Then he examined the suit and shirt.

"Are they—where did they come from?" Denis asked fearfully.

Clem had the brown cotton shirt in his hands. He explained that the clothes had been found by the curé of a small church ten miles from La Baie, found in the church.

"I asked Dulac to have his brother, who lives down that way, question some of the habitants. It seems one of them knew the old curé who found the bundle."

"They are—Jarret's, aren't they?" said Denis.

"The shirt is, I think. But I've never seen the suit. Looks new and probably was, because it's not soiled, only rumpled. Moreover, there's not a stain on it," he muttered more to himself than to her.

"I'm sure it is the suit he wore on the train," said Denis. "And there is no tie, you notice," she added significantly.

Clem gave her an amused glance. "Do you mean to imply that Jarret was strangled with the tie by a baker of Trois Lacs who is now wearing it?" He shook his head. "Only a ghoul would do that. Or a fool. No, there must be some other explanation."

"You don't think anything happened to Jarret?" Denis persisted anxiously.

"Certainly not in this suit, which hasn't a stain or even mud on it. But——" Clem hesitated and then said quickly, "We can't even be sure the suit was Jarret's. You say he wore it on the train but perhaps it was only one that looked like this."

Clem picked up the brown shirt again and examined it thoughtfully. "Hmm! You say his tie was yellow?"

"Yes and it had a spot that was exactly the shape of a beetle."

"And the Frenchman's yellow tie had a beetle, too, eh?" Clem grinned at her but sobered immediately and said that he certainly would have a talk with the man.

"But everything closes up in Trois Lacs on Monday so it would be useless to look for him today. I'll hunt him up tomorrow. Meanwhile——"

Clem rubbed his chin and scowled at the tweed suit. With his father away the clothes were his responsibility. He had meant to get the fence in the lower field mended today but it would have to wait.

"Meanwhile," he decided after a long minute of thought, "I'm afraid Uncle Duncan must identify these things before anything else can be done. He got back last night and since Dad isn't here I guess I'll have to drive over to Wickham Vale with them."

He had found some better string and was already rewrapping the suit and shirt. As he tied the package securely Denis remembered the knife she had slipped into the coat pocket.

"Oh, wait," she cried and explained about the knife, describing it as best she could.

"Sounds as though it might be Jarret's. But I'll have to take these things over to his father anyway, so there's no use opening the bundle again. Ever see an asbestos mine?" he added abruptly.

Denis shook her head.

"Get your coat and come along then," said Clem. "You're going to see one today."

CHAPTER VIII

A Special Sample

"THAT IS Wickham Vale, over there," said Clem.

He slowed up and pointed across country to what appeared from the distance to be the usual French Canadian village. The characteristic church spire rose from a cluster of houses between low hills and there was nothing to indicate the presence of the mine. It was hidden from view by one of the hills, along with the settlement of Fraserville where the mine employees lived, Clem explained as he drove on.

Although the village seemed near, looking across the fields, actually by road it was twelve miles away. Would Wickham Vale, picturesque from a distance, prove as commonplace as most of the villages through which they had come, Denis wondered. But when Clem turned off the main highway their road wound through prettier country until, just before they reached the village, the mine came into view.

"Oh!" said Denis in a shocked tone as she gazed at the great hole that was the asbestos mine, glaring white in the midday sun. "I thought you said it was a hill," she murmured at last.

"So it was, a pretty green hill—once."

Clem drove through the village, and down the half mile to the mine property entrance and stopped at the office where the superintendent, introduced as Mark Koppel, said that Uncle Duncan was up at the observation hut with someone.

"He just 'phoned for me. So if you want to go up, I'll ride along with you."

There had been a message from Jarret, he confided on the way. "The boy rang up this morning, said he was fine and rang off before his father could say a word. But Mr. Fraser looks better already. He had the call traced immediately and it came from Quebec."

"Quebec!" Clem said in surprise. "What would Jarret be doing there?"

"His father seems relieved just to be sure he's alive," said the older man.

Denis gave Clem an anxious glance but his attention was concentrated on the last steep piece of road. At the top of the hill he pulled up near the observation hut, switched off his motor and looked at the bundle between Denis and himself.

"You bet," he said with feeling. "So am I."

The superintendent went into the hut and Clem led Denis around to the observation platform overlooking the mine, in order that she might see it while they waited for Uncle Duncan to finish his business.

Far below was the gaping hole, two or three city blocks across, like a deep white crater. It shelved down in a series of rock terraces to a depth, according to Clem, of over three hundred and fifty feet. A train of open freight cars filled with chunks of rock chugged along one shelf, a train made by the distance to seem a mere toy, and on a lower shelf open cars were being loaded by a great electric shovel. Over everything in sight lay a fine white dust.

Instinctively Denis shuddered as she looked down.

"Quite a sight, eh?" said Clem without enthusiasm. "And it used to be a farm."

"Doesn't look much like one now, does it? Finest single asbestos mine in the world," Uncle Duncan boasted proudly as he joined them.

Denis looked from the mine to the man beside her. His gaze embraced the yawning crater below as a mother might watch her only child. The same cocky little man, his self-assurance had momentarily given way to the greater importance of the mine.

"Mark tell you I had a call from that crazy boy of mine? To wish me a happy birthday, if you please. Well, at least he's alive and safe. Now maybe——" He sighed, his gaze strayed back to the mine.

"Glad you brought Denis over, Clem. Ever see an asbestos

mine before, young lady? No? I suppose you thought asbestos was manufactured, eh? Well, what do you think of it?"

"It's so—big. And deep," said Denis inadequately. She had thought mines were always underground. What happened in winter?

"Gets pretty cold down on the lowest level," Uncle Duncan admitted. "But the men around here are used to cold."

"Do they work outside in winter?"

The man nodded proudly. "Day and night, winter and summer," he said and pointed out the search lamps that lighted the great hole for the night shift.

Pleased by her obvious interest, he answered her questions in such detail that Clem smiled to himself. And even to Denis it was apparent that her uncle was at his best showing off his mine. He knew every inch of it. He told her how many tons were taken out in a day by the train of cars that was now chugging up the last level on its way out of the mine. He pointed out sections where they had found little or no asbestos and promised that she would find the process of separating the asbestos from the rock almost as interesting as the mine itself.

When he explained that as soon as a section had been mined the tracks for the loading train were taken up and laid down in another place, Denis listened wide-eyed. Like everything else about the great hole, the idea of moving railroad tracks here and there seemed a marvel.

Why was there so much sand, or what looked like sand, on the stretch directly below the observation platform? was her next question.

"That's where we've finished mining a section and filled it in," the man explained. Although there was sand anyway, in places, some of it quicksand. They had to be careful.

Denis pointed to a rectangular patch of ground on which diminutive figures moved about, making dark, round spots. From the distance they might have been tufting a giant's quilt.

"What are those tiny men doing?" she asked curiously.

Duncan Fraser permitted himself a faint snort of amusement. "They are quite ordinary men. They do look like pygmies from here though," he admitted and explained that the men were setting dynamite in order to open up that particular section. The man in charge of the hut had come out and he turned to speak to him.

Since Clem was talking to Mark Koppel, Denis watched the electric shovel that had been loading rock into the freight cars and was now moving around the shelf. While she watched, it reached a sandy place and stopped. Idly she wondered why, since there were no rocks at that point to be loaded. Was it moving on? No, the driver leaned out and must have shouted to the workmen beyond for they dropped their tools and ran toward the big machine.

Suddenly Uncle Duncan broke off in the middle of what he had been saying, his attention drawn to the electric shovel far below. His sharp gaze followed the movements of the men for little more than a minute before he began to give orders, orders that sent Mark Koppel to a telephone on the run.

"I'll have to leave you," he told Clem and Denis. "They've hit quicksand. That shovel's sinking—and fast. Stop at the office on your way out. I'll have one of our special samples of asbestos there for Denis. Have to take her through the plant another day."

He had already started at a trot for his car and Clem hurried after him.

"But Uncle Duncan, one reason we came over—— Now you have heard from Jarret it isn't so important but——"

By the time Denis caught up with them, Clem had taken the bundle of clothes out of the car and Uncle Duncan was impatiently ripping it open. Yes, that was Jarret's shirt and his suit, a new one he had worn the day they started for Montreal.

"But why the dickens did he leave it in a church?" Duncan Fraser demanded with a bewildered shake of the head.

"You are sure the suit is Jarret's?" said Clem, while Denis reached into a pocket for the knife.

The older man's nod was emphatic. "Of course. And it's a darn good thing I know he's alive or I'd be worried sick. "What now?" he demanded irritably when an exclamation of dismay escaped Denis.

"It isn't there," she murmured and in response to the man's look of impatience explained that there had been a pocket knife in the suit.

"It must have dropped out when I put the things in the closet," she admitted, recalling how hastily she had rewrapped the bundle.

"Anyway these are Jarret's and I've got to get along. Thank heaven the boy's all right." Uncle Duncan grabbed the suit and started again for his car, calling back, "The men are in trouble with that shovel. I must get down to them."

He jumped in beside Mark Koppel and they were off before Clem and Denis could even wave good-by. But when Clem stopped at the office a few minutes later someone brought out the sample of asbestos. It was in a big, sealed manila envelope which Denis did not open but held absently on her lap until they turned into the main road ten minutes later.

"We'll have to find a place to eat now," Clem grumbled. "Ordinarily Uncle Duncan would have given us lunch and he has a whiz of a cook. But with one of his electric shovels in quicksand he won't even think of food."

"He loves the mine, doesn't he? And Clem, I'm pretty sure I know now why Jarret ran away."

"Why?" Clem demanded, his eyes on the road.

"Because he hated the mine. I can see how he might. It's wonderful to see, but imagine living there, working there!" She shuddered at the thought.

"Naturally a girl wouldn't like it but—— I wouldn't myself," he admitted after a pause. "And it's true that Jarret is crazy about the woods. But I never heard him say he disliked the mine. In fact I can't recall hearing him even speak of it."

"Don't you see why? Because he hated it. That's why he couldn't stick college. You should have seen his face when he was talking with Uncle Duncan that day on the station platform at Côte L'Avenir. He knew if he ever learned to be a mining engineer he was lost, tied to the mine forever," she finished triumphantly.

Clem said slowly, "You may be right. Because of course his father would want Jarret to take over the mine some day and Uncle Duncan is as stubborn as six mules, never can see anybody else's point of view."

Denis had ripped open the manila envelope and was examining the piece of greenish grey stone it contained. The rock was covered with a long white fuzz which apparently came from the shiny, splinter-like tubes that coated it.

Clem glanced at her and grinned. "Didn't you ever see natural asbestos before? Curious that the stuff should come out of the earth like that, isn't it?"

"It's remarkable," said Denis.

"He has given you an unusual sample. The ordinary visitor gets a small chunk with a bit of the white stuff clinging to it."

Denis continued to turn the stone over in her hands before she confided thoughtfully, "The strange thing is that the man with the yellow tie had a piece just this shape. And wouldn't it be natural for Jarret to have had one of his father's special samples?"

Clem whistled. "It would, indeed," he agreed. And no doubt Jarret had exchanged his clothes at La Baie for garments in which he would be less conspicuous. But how did a baker of Trois Lacs come to have, not the suit, but his yellow tie and the asbestos sample?

"I'll hunt up that Frenchman tomorrow," Clem announced. Although there was probably some simple explanation since Jarret was alive and all right. In fact, if Jarret had run away because he hated the mine and was not in trouble he, Clem, saw no reason to worry about him.

Denis continued to handle the asbestos sample, intrigued by its extraordinary combination of hard rock and soft cotton feeling. Her dislike of Uncle Duncan had undergone a change and she could not help feeling a little sorry for him. In spite of his pompous air, he had the unqualified respect of his men, she had noted. And in an emergency his one thought had been to join them. His love of the mine was so genuine that it seemed a pity Jarret did not share it.

What did Jarret want to try before he consented to study mining engineering—if he ever did? Why hadn't she questioned him when she had the opportunity? Denis frowned at the long straight road ahead and at last turned to Clem.

"Does it seem odd to you that Jarret should have called his father this morning?"

Clem shook his head. "No. The fact that his father was worrying about him on a birthday would bother Jarret. He's that kind of boy, as stubborn as Uncle Duncan in some ways, but more sensitive to other people's feelings."

They rode a mile or two in silence before Denis said, "But suppose—it wasn't Jarret?"

Clem scoffed at the notion. Was she suggesting that Duncan Fraser could not recognize his own son's voice?

Denis started to reply, thought better of it, then changed her mind again and spoke.

"Hello? Hello, Dad. Happy birthday. Don't worry about me, I'm getting on fine," she said.

Her inflection and tone of voice were such an amazing counterpart of Jarret's that Clem pulled the car over to the side of the road, switched off the motor and turned to her in unbelief.

"Great Guns! It's uncanny," he exclaimed. "You only talked to him for a few minutes on a train. I've heard grandfather imitate people but never quite as well as that. It's a gift."

Denis laughed and thought of the many times she had imitated someone's voice or manner only to be stopped by her mother, who strongly disapproved of what Clem called a gift. She reminded him that her father was an actor and if her grandfather as well had ability along that line it was not so strange she should, too. Music had taught her to recognize even the slightest variation in tone, she pointed out.

But Clem said that did not explain what he considered an uncanny talent. Why, it was positively spooky. If she intended to imply that someone other than Jarret had telephoned, however, she was wrong.

"Your voice was perfect. But never, since he was a baby, has Jarret called his father anything but Dunky, although he always speaks of him as father to strangers. He must have said Dunky over the 'phone. Uncle Duncan would have been suspicious at once of anything else," Clem declared.

"Oh," said Denis. "Then he is probably all right."

"Yes, I don't think we need worry now. And perhaps we'll know more when I've talked to that baker in Trois Lacs, found where he got the asbestos and the tie," Clem added as he drove on.

But it did seem strange that Jarret should have telephoned the very morning his suit turned up, Denis pondered. And what was he "trying" in Quebec? Odd that knife should have dropped out of the suit, although of course she had tossed the bundle into the closet hastily in her anxiety to get it out of sight. Jeanpierre had seen its contents and probably recognized the knife, but he seemed a discreet boy. Her random thoughts lingered on Jeanpierre long enough to remind her of something else and Denis turned to Clem.

"Was Jarret interested in music?" she asked impulsively.

Clem, who had just announced that there was a place in the next town where they could get something to eat, expected an enthusiastic response. And she had not even heard him. He gave her a startled glance.

"Music? Gosh, I don't know. He plays by ear; always played for us when we wanted to sing 'Alouette' or 'Roulant Ma Boule'. But if you mean seriously interested, I'm pretty sure not. I never saw any evidence of it."

So it was not music Jarret wanted to try. What was it?

CHAPTER IX

Tracks Across the Pond

IF FRENCH CANADA was as cold as this in November what must it be in January? Denis shivered, fumbled for a match with stiff fingers and scurried back into bed to watch the fire blaze up cozily. This was the third day she had needed one and Clem promised skating if the temperature continued to fall.

"You'll have to skate, you know, Dee. And ski later on. You're supposed to stay out-of-doors. Remember?"

But Denis was learning to return Clem's shots. "I could build a snowman," she had retorted.

As it happened, Lawrence Fraser had taught his small daughter to skate almost as soon as she could walk, so while she had had little opportunity of practice in recent years when all her free hours were spent at the piano, Denis would not be a complete novice. Skiing was another matter. But Claire said Jeanpierre could teach anyone to ski.

Jeanpierre! As she snuggled under the blankets watching the fire, Denis wondered about the French boy. Could he have taken the pocketknife out of Jarret's suit? He knew the bundle was in the closet and had had the opportunity when he brought in the second load of wood. And if Jeanpierre had not taken the knife, where could it be? They had not found it in the hall closet.

Clem insisted it would probably turn up, might be in the suit after all, and he no longer seemed concerned about Jarret. Even his discovery that the baker of Trois Lacs had gone to La Baie where he was supposed to have a sick mother—La Baie of all places—did not bother Clem. Since the telephone call from Quebec he seemed satisfied that Jarret was in no danger and would work things out for himself. But until the baker's return the question of how the man came into possession of

Jarret's tie and asbestos sample remained as puzzling as the disappearance of the knife.

When Denis reluctantly emerged from her warm nest at last, there was just time to whip into her clothes, for Aunt Felice not only expected everyone to be at the breakfast table but to be there promptly. When she slid into her chair the clock was striking eight and the others were there; all but Midge. Angelica was often late when she was at home but it was so unusual for Midge not to be on time that Denis immediately asked if she were sick.

"Margot will spend the day locked in her room alone," Aunt Felice replied briefly, her attention on pouring the chocolate.

It was Claire who explained, while Denis forgot breakfast in her concern. She had known that Midge's little visitor of the day before had managed to get them both into mischief and that somehow the crow had flown into the house. But now, it seemed, the Laurent family ring was gone. The ring was kept in a small enamel box on one of the tables in the living room, but Aunt Felice had been showing it to the children just before the crow flew in. She had put it down hastily as she jumped up and after Jeanpierre finally got the crow out, after the excitement was over, she had thought of the ring again. And it was not on the table, nor in the chair, nor on the floor. The ring had vanished.

"Do you think Tommy Trimmer picked it up?" Clem asked.

Aunt Felice thought not, naughty as Midge's visitor was. "It would not be the first thing that wretched crow has stolen," she declared. "It was only a day or two after the last time he got into the house that we found your grandfather's gold pencil gone, the pencil he likes to use when he changes a music score."

"But, Ma Tante, we don't know the crow took it," Clem protested.

"We know he is a thief. Also the pencil was on your grandfather's desk and then it was gone. And no one in the house would have touched it," Aunt Felice finished in her most decisive way.

The crow? Denis had looked up astonished, then hastily occupied herself with her eggs as she remembered that it was Jeanpierre who got rid of the crow. Was the French boy as trustworthy as they all thought? Certainly no crow had taken Jarret's knife.

"I thought Mr. Crow had left us for the winter," said Clem. "How did he get in anyway?"

"How did everything happen yesterday?" Aunt Felice wondered.

Claire said hastily, "It was that fiendish Tommy Trimmer who let the little pigs out you know, Mama. Midge was only trying to catch them when she upset the flower pots."

"And when Curly Rose was locked in the fruit cellar? And they cut all the crusts off the fresh bread? Did Midge try to capture little pigs then?" With a frown of distaste Aunt Felice said she did not wish to recall all the naughty things they had done. The worst of it was that Tommy Trimmer had been invited because she thought Midge was depending too much on animals and should have the companionship of a child her own age.

Clem restrained a smile when her mother added vehemently that the visitor was *un petit bête*.

She was driving to Trois Lacs this morning with Uncle Guy and taking Curly Rose to the dentist, Aunt Felice announced a few minutes later. Before they left she would take Margot some bread and milk. "But you understand, Claire? She is to have nothing else. Also, she may not have the dogs with her."

Claire nodded miserably and there was an uncomfortable silence, for Denis was not the only one fond of Midge, who was her father's favorite and Clem's special weakness. At last breakfast was over and they scattered to separate tasks.

Denis rushed upstairs, determined to find some way of comforting Midge if the opportunity offered and meanwhile anxious to finish her chores and join Claire who had promised to give her a cooking lesson. She made her bed, gave the room a hurried dusting and stepped into the hall just in time to see Aunt Felice locking Midge's door.

Impulsively Denis went back. She could not smuggle one of the dogs in to Midge, much as she would have liked to, but there was something she could do. Across a sheet of paper she printed a message.

I don't believe the crow took the ring. We'll find it—D.

Quietly she tiptoed to the child's door and slid the paper under it. Although she was risking the serious disapproval of Aunt Felice if caught, Denis felt much happier as she ran downstairs with Nicolette. Instinct told her that Midge would take punishment for any other mischief philosophically but would be heartbroken over the loss of Grandfather's ring.

That the crow had snatched it up seemed preposterous. Surely he would have been too confused by the efforts of several people to get rid of him. And the more she thought about it the less likely it seemed that Jeanpierre had taken a valuable ring even if he was responsible for the missing knife. Had Tommy Trimmer picked up the ring? Or had—— There was another possibility, thought Denis, as she found a coat and stepped out on the back gallery to give the dogs a run.

In spite of the cold, Jeanpierre was working on something down near the kitchen end, singing as usual. When she saw that he was whittling a piece of wood, Denis realized that this was her opportunity to bring up the subject of the pocket-knife. While Nicolette and Charcoal chased each other around the house she approached the French boy. He had stopped singing and was humming absently to himself, absorbed in his tasks when Denis paused a few feet from him to listen.

"What is that song?" she demanded suddenly.

Jeanpierre looked up at her blankly.

"*Qu'est-ce que vous chantez?*" Denis urged and when he only shook his head in a puzzled fashion, she began to hum the tune herself.

But he showed no recognition of it and when finally made to understand that she wanted him to repeat something he had been singing, Jeanpierre thought a minute and then began to sing another tune. Whether or not he was deliberately misleading her she did not know, but he could not be persuaded to sing the air again.

Exasperated, Denis called the dogs and went into the house, realizing too late that in her desire to track down that tantalizing strain of music she had heard the day they went fishing, she had completely forgotten to question the French boy about Jarret's knife. How stupid! Well, at least she could hum the thing now and perhaps Claire would know what song it came from.

But Claire, busy kneading the bread dough, looked as blank as Jeanpierre when Denis hummed the melody.

"It's familiar, yet it isn't," said Claire. "Wash your hands and I'll show you how to set a pan of rolls."

While the rolls were rising Claire made an apple pie. She sliced the tart crab apples very thin and sweetened them with maple sugar. Then she showed Denis how to make the pastry, cutting the cold shortening into the flour and rolling it out so deftly that the tasks seemed simple. She was making a cheese omelette for lunch and Denis was watching closely because, as she wrote her mother, Claire's omelettes were simply dreamy, when Clem came in.

"Smells good and I'm starved. We can skate on Birch Lake this afternoon," he added as he pulled off his sweater. "Want to go?"

If her mother returned in time, Claire agreed. Otherwise she could not leave the house, not with Midge alone upstairs.

"And I have no skates," Denis objected.

"Let's see your foot. That's easy. You can probably wear Jarret's old skates," Clem told her.

But after lunch when he looked for the skates they were not to be found.

"That's strange. I'm sure I saw them here only a few days ago when I got my own out to be sharpened. I'll look again."

Clem ducked back into the hall closet reserved for skates and skis and snowshoes but could find only figure skates belonging to his cousin. "I suppose I didn't see them," he said doubtfully at last.

"You don't think the crow took them?" Denis asked innocently.

Clem gave her a quizzical glance and then laughed. "Well, they make the third thing that's disappeared so we don't have to worry about anything else, eh?"

In the end Claire used the figure skates and loaned Denis hers which fortunately proved to be an excellent fit.

It seemed incredible that afternoon to find Birch Lake, across which they had paddled but a few weeks ago, a solid sheet of ice. Clem admitted that the lake was rarely frozen hard so early. "That's why we might as well take advantage of it," he said.

When Denis watched Claire glide easily into a forward eight and out of it into a spiral, she wondered whether she could even skate around the lake. But after the first awkward minute she fould herself striking out confidently beside Clem.

"I thought I might have forgotten what to do," she admitted.

"Never. It's like swimming or driving a car. You don't forget." Figure skating was another matter, of course, and meant constant practice. "Want to see Hidden Pond?" he demanded suddenly, after they had circled the lake twice.

They left Claire trying a double spin and picked their way through the narrow channel that led to the pond. In places a rocky wall rose on either side of them and the channel, actually a stony brook, was anything but smooth. Fortunately it was not long before they were stopped by several strands of barbed wire stretched across the Pond end of the brook.

"But anyone could scramble up the bank and then down the hill beyond the wire," Denis objected.

Clem agreed that the only real use of the wire, especially

in winter, was as a sort of keep-off sign. "It's Jules Dulac's way of saying he doesn't want anybody on the pond."

"Dulac? Is he related to Jeanpierre?"

"Yes, a distant cousin. I suppose Jeanpierre might get away with fishing or skating on the pond, but I wouldn't want to try it."

Hidden Pond was certainly well named, thought Denis, as she looked at the steep hills, dark with fir and spruce, that enclosed it on all but one side. It was like a deep green cup with a piece broken out of one side and a layer of ice over the bottom. Where the cup was broken, stood the old stone tower Clem had told her about, so close to the water that the ice seemed to curve halfway around the base. The tower was round and about thirty feet high, with narrow slits or windows in the upper part. Back of it the ground sloped gradually

up to what appeared to be a great pile of stones and a wall partially screened by a huge fir balsam.

That was the old *château*, all that was left of it, Clem explained. Jules Dulac had built himself a kind of shack against the north end which was not completely ruined. "You can't see his house from here because of the tree but he can see the pond, you may be sure."

The tower, so close to the pond that in summer the water must lap against its stone wall, was like something out of a fairy story. How many years had passed since a human being

had been inside? As her gaze moved on up the slope to the ruin, Denis said impulsively, "There must have been some entrance. Why has no one found it?"

"Because it's probably buried under that pile of stones," Clem said. "That end of the *château* was nearest to the tower so it stands to reason that's where the entrance to any secret passage would be."

"I wonder——" Denis stopped.

"Why Jarret and I didn't move the stones, I suppose," said Clem, adding that a girl would have some such crazy notion and after all they had come out to skate not to moon over an old tower.

"You haven't a chance of getting into it unless you can learn to fly. So come along," he told her.

But Denis could not forget the mysterious tower and when, a little later, Clem and Claire left her to rest on a log near the channel while they tried a double eight together, she could not resist the temptation to go back. It was harder to pick her way over the rough brook without help but she had covered half the distance when she stopped suddenly, almost losing her balance. Someone was whistling the melody Jeanpierre had refused to sing for her, someone on Hidden Pond.

Denis started off again in such haste that a few yards from the end of the channel she crashed into a dead branch and only by throwing herself against the bank escaped a bad fall. The whistling ceased. When she reached the barbed wire, Hidden Pond was as deserted as it had been earlier in the afternoon and the old tower stood grey and mysterious across the ice. Was the whistler inside? Excited by the possibility, Denis stared intently at the narrow openings in the stone wall. But no sound, or movement or any sign of life rewarded her.

The sun had disappeared behind the hills leaving a penetrating cold in the green cup. Since there was nothing to be gained by staring at the tower, Denis shivered and was about to turn reluctantly back when, with a startled gasp, she noticed the ice. All over the pond ran the tracks of a skater, a good skater; even she could see that.

Of course it must have been Jeanpierre because Clem had said old Jules would permit no one else to use the pond. But why had he vanished when he heard the racket she made? And the song? Why had he pretended not to know it that morning? Denis returned to the lake more puzzled than ever. What was this song that no one knew or would admit knowing?

CHAPTER X

A Challenge

THE THERMOMETER hovered around ten above zero for another week and Denis acquired some skates of her own. With
either Claire, Midge, Clem or all three she spent a part of
almost every day at Birch Lake, but only once did she manage to escape the others long enough to make her way over the
frozen channel to Hidden Pond.

No glimpse of Jeanpierre rewarded her and no sound broke
the stillness. Across the ice the stone tower remained provok-
ingly mysterious. There were only the tracks of a skater to
prove someone actually had whistled that melody so befitting
the place. Denis knew enough now to realize that the tracks
had been made by a figure skater and a good one, so there
seemed little doubt that Jeanpierre was responsible for them.
But his pretence of not knowing the song remained as puzzling
as the disappearance of Jarret's knife. The skating had been
wonderful, however, and she was even beginning to think of
trying figure skates.

"You look more alive than you did when you first came,"
Clem informed her in his outspoken fashion as they trudged
back from the lake on the last afternoon before the thaw.
Claire had gone horseback riding with Bruce Walker and
Midge was getting over a cold. If she was not well enough to
go to the convent she could not go skating, Aunt Felice had
decreed.

The afternoons were short now, the light fading quickly
after the sun had set, and it would be dusk by the time Denis
and Clem got to the house. When they were still a quarter of
a mile from the Manor, a horse and buggy loomed up ahead,
moving toward them.

"Looks like—— Yes, I thought that grey nag was familiar,

it's old Jules Dulac," said Clem. "And he has someone with him. Wait here for them to pass, eh?" he added, stepping to the side of the road.

But the old Frenchman pulled up his horse and spoke to Clem, his deep voice booming over the quiet road. Denis could make little of what he said except that it had something to do with a dog. Yet her desire to get into the tower on Hidden Pond made her interested in the man himself, what the dim light revealed of him. He was big, his shoulders and even his arms and hands were broad. When he pulled off a mitten and blew his nose on a large red handkerchief, she saw that they were the powerful hands of a rugged man who had spent most of his life in the open. He looked capable of moving the pile of stones that Clem said must conceal a passage entrance to the tower, of moving the whole ruined *château* in fact, by himself. Strange that he had not done so.

His companion was but a vague, silent figure on the far side of the buggy. All she could see of the man was that under

an old felt hat he wore a black patch over one eye. Yet once she thought he chuckled at something Clem said, and when old Jules finally shrugged and gave the horse a go-ahead slap with the reins, his companion raised a hand in parting salute, even in its heavy leather glove a much smaller hand than that of old Jules.

"You didn't tell me he was such a powerful man," she said as they walked on.

"I told you very few people had seen Hidden Pond," said Clem. "It remains hidden because men just don't argue with Jules Dulac, even those half his age."

"What did he say about *mon chien?*"

"He wanted to know if I'd seen his dog. It has been gone two days and he thought it might have wandered down here." Clem shook his head in disapproval and said the trouble was that old Jules sometimes went off for a few days leaving the dog to shift for himself and then was surprised if it wandered off.

"Oh," said Denis and walked on beside Clem in thoughtful silence until they were almost home. Then she asked, "Who was the man with him?"

"I haven't the faintest idea. I suppose Jules Dulac has some cronies, although most of the habitants dislike him. I've seen them shake their heads when Grandfather, who likes to hear old Jules play his fiddle, said a good word for him."

They had reached the house where Clem gave his skates to Denis and went straight on to the barn. She put them away with her own in the closet and hung her leather jacket and hood in the other closet. Jules Dulac was sometimes away from home, she had learned, and such an absence would be her opportunity to search for an entrance to the tower on Hidden Pond.

In the living room the lamps were lighted but it was not until she reached the fire that Denis discovered Uncle Duncan in one of the big wing chairs and Midge in the other. Uncle Duncan, it seemed, had stopped for the night on his way home from Quebec where he had spent several days trying to locate

Jarret. He looked years older than the pompous little man she had first seen on the station at Côte L'Avenir.

"If only I could find the boy and——" He checked himself, staring helplessly into the fire.

Shorn of his domineering manner, Uncle Duncan was curiously pathetic, the more so because Denis sensed he was no longer in the mood to dictate, that if Jarret were there his father would be willing to compromise on the college question or anything else. Jarret must be found, she decided impulsively, if only that he could be told of his father's changed attitude.

Midge seemed maddeningly unperturbed by the fact that her uncle could not find Jarret. She looked almost too innocent as she sat feeding nuts to the chipmunk who was stuffing most of them into his cheek pouches for future use. Denis, wishing she could read the child's mind, warmed her hands and sought for some comforting thing to say to Uncle Duncan. She could think of nothing that would not sound fatuous but she remembered a question she wanted to ask.

"What about the electric shovel that sank into the quicksand? Did you get it out?" she asked.

The man's face brightened. "We did. But we had to take the thing apart and then borrow a crane from the railroad to do it. You see——" He broke off and frowned at her thoughtfully.

"Do you know, I hadn't noticed it before but you are very like Lawrence. Oh, not in looks, because Larry was the image of Father." He glanced at the portrait above the fire. "But in manner, the way you use your hands and something about the way you speak. As a boy, Larry used to—— Ah, here is tea."

Aunt Felice had come in followed by Curly Rose with the tea tray and Uncle Duncan stood up, leaving Denis to wonder what he had been going to say about her father for whom his tone betrayed a deep affection. Yet he had tried to keep him from the one thing Lawrence Fraser wanted to do. Why? Why, when it meant that he never saw her father again? Suddenly, the knowledge that he had been fond of her father and the way he kept looking at the portrait of Denis Laurent as though for once he wanted advice, enlisted her sympathy.

Jarret must be found. If she couldn't get anything out of Midge and Clem wasn't interested, she must find him herself.

Denis smiled absently at Uncle Guy when he joined them with the dogs, nibbled a third cookie and looked up at the portrait herself. She had the strangest feeling that in her grandfather's laughing black eyes there was a clue to Jarret's whereabouts—if only she could read it. The others were talking and she was so preoccupied with her own thoughts that she was only vaguely aware of Jeanpierre when he brought more wood for the fire. She did not see Clem come in nor hear what they were saying until the sound of her own name made her jump.

"But Dee could play for him. Couldn't you, Dee?" Midge begged.

"Play?"

When Midge explained that Jeanpierre would sing if someone would play the piano, Denis stared at her in dismay. The child's cold, added to her distress over the loss of the heirloom ring, had given her face a pinched look that bothered Denis. Since her own hope of finding the ring was fading, she would like to make it up to Midge in some way. But the piano——

They were all looking at her. She sat, painfully aware of Clem's mocking blue eyes and Midge's pleading gaze, before Uncle Guy came to the rescue.

"Denis is not supposed to practice this winter, you see, Midge. And I doubt if she knows the songs," he explained.

Clem added, "And music is far too important for her to bother with the folk songs of French Canada."

His tone was reasonable enough but his quizzical expression was a taunt Denis couldn't ignore. When at Midge's crestfallen look, Clem said never mind maybe he could pick out an accompaniment himself, she stood up.

"Certainly I'll play, Midge, if the music is there."

Denis started toward the piano, thankful that her years of practice had made it so easy to read music and knowing that her only difficulty would be to get the proper rhythm. Then, after Clem found the book of Canadian songs and she glanced over the first one Jeanpierre picked out, it occurred to her that the illusive melody of Hidden Pond might be among them. Or if it was not in the book, she might play by ear the little she knew and thus trap the French boy into singing it.

After they had sung *En Roulant Ma Boule* and *Youpé! Youpé! Sur La Rivière,* and several others, Midge asked for *Alouette.* While Clem hunted out the music for that, Denis touched the piano keys softly, fumbling for the mysterious melody, all she could remember.

"What name has this song, Jeanpierre?" she asked and repeated the question in French, looking up at him unexpectedly while she played.

Jeanpierre's face took on a completely blank expression and he shook his head. "Heem I know not."

But of course he did know it. Hadn't she heard him whistling the thing? Why was he so secretive about it? Exasperated, Denis began to play "Alouette." They all knew that and they all sang, even Uncle Duncan. But three verses did not satisfy Midge.

"Just once more," she begged.

An amusing thought struck Denis who had not joined in the singing but liked the songs; their gaiety and humor were contagious, the rhythm was fun. "I'll sing it as—as Clem would," she offered impetuously.

"A-lou-et-te, gen-tille A-lou-et-te——"

It was her turn to give Clem a mocking glance as she imitated his voice and mannerisms. While they all laughed she began the refrain again softly in her own voice and then suddenly it was old Jules Dulac singing.

Midge would have kept her at the piano all night but Aunt Felice said Jeanpierre had to go home, and also Denise must be tired, and it was almost time for supper.

"I didn't know you could sing," Claire said as Denis closed the piano.

"I can't. I have very little voice."

"But it has a quality; you have the flair. And the imitations were—— Yes, Mamma, I am coming."

She hurried off, leaving Denis with the appalling thought— imitations! Just what she was not supposed to do. As for the French songs, undoubtedly they would come under the heading of popular music which she never had been allowed to play. She did not know Clem was still there until he spoke, beginning where Claire had left off.

"And the imitations were—swell. You gave a lot of people pleasure just now, Dee. You may be right about music, after all."

Denis looked at him helplessly. "But it wasn't——"

Clem's shrewd blue eyes read her thought. "It wasn't im-

portant," he finished. "You enjoyed it, though, didn't you? What's the use of being important if you don't enjoy it?"

"You know all the answers, don't you?" said Denis. "Maybe you can tell me the name of the song I tried to play for Jeanpierre."

"Never heard it. And all I'm trying to say is that you forgot your possible importance as a pianist just now and you were—well, I think you were swell."

"Oh!" said Denis. She no longer was disconcerted by Clem's big-brother advice and was growing accustomed to his frank comments but they had not prepared her for a compliment.

"Oh!" Then she laughed. "And if you think so I suppose that settles it. But—thanks, Clem."

CHAPTER XI

Friday the Thirteenth

"I'M GOING to straighten out the music cabinet," Claire announced the next morning.

It was badly in need of attention she had noticed yesterday, and who could tell—her grandfather might come home suddenly and not be able to find what he wanted. The truth was that Claire, like her mother, had a passionate love of order.

"Here's another Gilbert and Sullivan operetta," she told Denis who had offered to help. "They all ought to be together. Grandfather always plays them when he feels gay."

Instead of putting the score of the *Mikado* with the others, however, Denis ruffled through it and presently began to run over the music.

> "A wandering minstrel I
> A thing of rags and patches . . ."

But the light, tuneful melodies did not make her feel gay, rather they increased the lost feeling that had taken possession of her. It was as though she had been clinging to something that kept her afloat and suddenly she had let go and was sinking. All very well for Clem to say she had given them pleasure by playing those Canadian songs and by imitating old Jules Dulac and the others. But that sort of thing had nothing to do with her because she was going to be a concert pianist. Of course she was.

> "—if patriotic sentiment is needed . . ."

Automatically Denis's fingers ran over the keys while she tried to forget the disturbing thoughts that possessed her. Was she just lazy? Was that why she so dreaded the hours and hours of practice that being a good pianist would mean? The alternative, that she was not destined to be a concert pianist after all, she could not face. Of course she was going to be a pianist and she need not think about the long hours of practice now because the doctor had forbidden them. She could just enjoy the piano this winter if she wanted to.

Denis scarcely realized that she still was playing snatches from the *Mikado* until Midge came in after a run with the dogs and begged her to sing. Aunt Felice, who was superstitious about Friday when it fell on the thirteenth, had decided that Midge need not go back to the convent until Monday, although she was well enough to be out.

"Sing, Dee. Please," Midge begged.

"It's too early in the morning for Dee to sing," Claire objected. "Besides, I'm ready to do the bench now."

Denis promptly stood up and opened the piano bench, noticing among its disorderly contents several pieces of music over which she had labored. When a book of Chopin's *Études* slipped to the floor, she picked it up with an inward shudder of distaste. After spending days and weeks learning one of the *études* in that book for the recital, she had never played it. And never wanted to.

Something fell out of the Chopin book as she picked it up. A snapshot.

"Why, it's Jarret," said Midge. "That was the Christmas he first——" She stopped.

Denis was thinking that the boy in the picture, with a pair of skates hung over his shoulder, was much younger than the Jarret she had met on the train. She looked up, wondering why Midge did not finish, and was as surprised as the others to see Angelica in the doorway.

Claire's astonishment immediately changed to suspicion. What was Angie doing at home on a Friday morning? Had anything happened? Claire demanded.

"A holiday happened," Angelica informed her sister gleefully as she joined them at the piano. And she had been lucky enough to get a ride home. "And I'm going to Quebec this afternoon. Marie Ruell is having a house party and Mamma says I may go. Can I take your yellow evening dress, Claire?"

"Angie! Have you spilled something on the pink taffeta Mamma made you? Or torn it?"

"Of course not. You know I don't spill things, Claire," Angelica said loftily. "It's just that I wore that one the last time I stayed at Marie's. Jack Ruell will think I have no other dress. What's that picture, Midge? Oh, Jarret! He certainly has grown up since that was taken. By the by, I hope Uncle Duncan hasn't caught up with him. No? Good. Claire, what about the dress?" Angie coaxed.

"I don't—know," said Claire. "Midge, do put that snapshot back when you and Angie finish looking at it. The picture must be one Grandfather particularly likes or he wouldn't keep it in his Chopin."

"The dress, Claire?" her sister urged.

"I don't know what to say, Angie. The yellow dress isn't your size. You cannot expect to wear a different dress to every party."

"But you said it was small for you and too short. And yellow's my color. Couldn't we try it on, anyway?"

Claire groaned and agreed, "Oh, I suppose it could be taken in. I'll see what I can do if Dee will bake the rolls. Curly Rose is cleaning upstairs today and they must be about ready to put in the oven. Add a good stick of wood to the fire," she warned when Denis eagerly consented to take over the baking.

"You're not learning to cook, Dee?" Angelica exclaimed in pretended horror. "What a mistake! Don't you know that once you learn things like that you'll be expected to do them?"

"What a lazy, pleasure-loving creature you are, Angie," said Claire. "Do give me that Chopin book, Midge," Denis heard her add as she started for the kitchen.

Proud to be trusted with the rolls, she put a stick of wood on the fire as instructed before she brushed the rolls with melted butter as she had seen Claire do and slid the pan into the oven. A wood stove presented problems, she had learned and the fire must be watched.

Denis watched it not as Claire would have done, with confident knowledge, but rather like a cat at a mouse hole, and when she ventured to open the oven door twenty minutes later, was a little surprised to find the rolls still there and apparently doing well. Just as she was wondering whether they were brown enough, Aunt Felice came in and gave them an appraising glance.

"Two minutes only and they will be *fini*. You have done well, Denise."

Two minutes later by the clock Denis took the rolls out, her cheeks flushed with pride as well as rosy from standing over the stove. She had used a pot holder but only one hand and it was a large pan of rolls, a very hot pan. Just before she reached the table with it the pan slipped out of her clutch and landed on the floor upside down.

Aunt Felice made a small sound of impatience before, with one of her rapid movements she snatched the pot holder from Denis, another from its hook, righted the pan and picked it up.

"Are they ruined?" Denis breathed miserably.

The older woman glanced at her and bit back a smile. "I think that no. A little squashed only. And you have learned that one must use two hands. Experience, it is the best teacher, *n'est-ce pas?*"

If Denise would run out to the barn and get some more eggs from Clem, Aunt Felice offered a few minutes later, she should learn to make a soufflé.

Denis was only too eager. She had had a narrow escape with the rolls, in which she felt an inordinate pride, considering that all she had done was put them in the oven, take them out and drop them. But she wanted to learn more. Cooking was fun. And at *Manoir Laurent* they made things that were so delicious.

Clem brought her down to earth. "Did you bring a dish for the eggs? I thought not. I'll have to find something for them." Then he relented. "I have news for you."

He had seen the baker of Trois Lacs, Clem admitted, and found out about the tie and the piece of asbestos.

"The Frenchman's name is Pelang and he comes from La

Baie where his mother still lives. It seems that one day in September—the day after Jarret disappeared it must have been because he said there had been a bad rain the day before—he was returning to Trois Lacs after visiting his mother. On one of the short cuts, a back road, he picked up a boy."

"Oh!" said Denis. "Then——"

"Wait, I haven't finished. The boy was dressed like any habitant in a plaid wool shirt, old trousers and——" Clem broke off as Jeanpierre came into that part of the barn. "I'll tell you later," he murmured.

Had the French boy heard what they were saying, Denis wondered, watching him out of the corner of her eyes as she took the eggs and said she had better hurry back to the house, that Aunt Felice would be waiting for them. Then, on a sudden impulse she turned back, raising her voice so that Jeanpierre, who had started to clean one of the stalls, could not fail to hear.

"Just the same I'd like to know what became of Jarret's pocketknife," said Denis unexpectedly and smiled to herself all the way back to the house over Clem's look of complete mystification.

There were crimson patches of excitement in Angelica's cheeks and her black eyes were bright with anticipation when Clem put her on the afternoon train for Quebec, along with her bag in which was carefully packed the yellow evening dress. She looked two or three years older than she was and very pretty.

"Sometimes Angelica seems older than Claire," said Denis.

"She is in a way. Angie was born wise about some things. She never would be taken in by that Bruce Walker. Not Angie," he added confidently.

"You don't like him, do you?"

"No, do you?" snapped Clem as he started his motor.

"I hadn't given it much thought. After all, he's Claire's affair."

"That's the trouble," Clem growled. "He shouldn't be. He's not Claire's dish at all. And I don't like it."

Her sidelong glance found him looking so grim that Denis wanted to laugh, although she did not think too much of Bruce Walker herself.

"You can't decide things for everybody, you know," she murmured slyly. "Tell me about the baker and Jarret."

Clem did not answer for a minute or two. He had turned into a side road because he wanted to stop in one of the hill villages on the way home to see a man about some wood, and from his scowl it was evident that he was still thinking of Claire and her latest date.

"What about Jarret?" Denis urged impatiently. "The baker picked up a boy dressed like a habitant——"

"Yes. Well, when they got to Trois Lacs, after spending one night in the cart, the boy said he couldn't pay much for the ride but he pulled a yellow silk necktie out of his pocket and gave the baker that along with an unusual stone."

Denis thought of the ticket receipt, still somewhere in the depths of her purse, the ticket to Trois Lacs. She sat up eagerly. "Clem, do you suppose he's right there in Trois Lacs and has been all the time?"

"You forget the telephone call Uncle Duncan traced. Besides it seems he told Pelang he was going to Quebec."

"Oh," said Denis, disappointed. Just the same, she thought, Jarret must have had some reason to buy a ticket to Trois Lacs. Why not one to Quebec?

As the narrow road wormed its way up into the hills, Denis was silent, mulling over the puzzle, while Clem concentrated on his driving. When he stopped at last she saw that it was a typical habitant village, almost as picturesque as those she had seen in paintings. There was a good skating rink and Clem parked his car near it, suggesting that Denis could watch the skaters while he hunted out the man he had come to see.

"If you get cold you can stay in the car. Too bad we couldn't find Midge in time to bring her along," Clem added. "She likes to come over here and watch these people skate."

Clem disappeared and Denis joined the bystanders along the ice, most of them old men and very young children. The skaters in their brightly colored caps and jackets flew about, up and down, in and out, making a colorful scene. A boy and girl flashed by, his red wool scarf streaming back beside her blue one. The watchers shouted approval of the way they kept in step, clapped when a lone Frenchman whirled into a good spin. Along the outskirts two or three older men glided sedately along, hands clasped behind them, undaunted by such stunts.

Denis understood why Midge liked to visit the habitant rink. It was simple and hearty and gay. Someone began to sing; others took it up and the skaters fell into the rhythm of the song. They did not seem conscious of the cold. Presently Denis noticed one skater who was better than all the others. He wore a red and yellow plaid shirt and knitted red cap with ear muffs and, although he skimmed about so fast she could not see his face, there was something familiar about him. She had seen Jeanpierre wear a shirt exactly like that and no doubt he had a red cap with ear muffs. The boy was doing some difficult jumps now and several of the skaters had drawn aside to watch.

"Bravo! Bravo!" they shouted when he executed a perfect spiral.

"Bravo!"

Denis turned when the man beside her took up the shout. He grinned in a friendly fashion. "Heem skate good, eh? *Il fait bien.*"

"*Oui, très bien.* What is his name?"

The Frenchman shrugged and shook his head. He didn't know the name. "Heem I know not. *C'est un visiteur.*"

The skater did not belong in the village then. Was it Jeanpierre? Eagerly Denis turned to find out, but the others were all darting about over the rink again and the boy in the red and yellow plaid shirt was no longer on the ice. Nor could she see him among the onlookers. She told Clem about the skater when he joined her a few minutes later, suggesting that it might be Jeanpierre, but Clem only laughed at her.

"Lots of the habitant boys are wonderful skaters and they like to try the different rinks. Why should it be Jeanpierre? Aren't you seeing him behind everything all of a sudden?"

"Maybe I am. But if he didn't take Jarret's knife, where can it be? You didn't take it out of the suit, did you?" she demanded.

A quizzical glance was her only answer.

"As for the boy on the rink, Miss Detective, it couldn't possibly have been Jeanpierre because he's at home, splitting wood. Or if not, he'll catch it from Dad. And so will I," Clem added grimly.

CHAPTER XII

The Wrong Direction

ONCE MORE Denis crossed the living room and gazed anxiously out one of the front windows. But there was no one in sight and the country looked bleak, lonesome and hopeless, as hopeless as she felt. Miserably she began to wander about the room again, pausing at last before the fireplace to gaze unhappily at the portrait of her grandfather. Nicolette, sensing that something was amiss, had been following her about and Denis stooped to rumple the poodle's topknot affectionately. A faint tinkle brought her up, alert. Was that the telephone at last?

No, it was only Mr. Chip in the glass nut dish on the table. Now he was down and had darted past her. Automatically Denis watched as he scurried around the wing chair over to the window and up the heavy overdrapery until he was about five feet from the floor. From that vantage he leaped to the pot of ivy on the stand in front of the window.

Although she had been watching for a week or more and suspected that he was building a second nest somewhere in the house, Denis had not found one nor had she ever seen him bury anything in the ivy before. Thus, when he had disposed of his treasure and scampered off, content, she walked over to investigate. She found the nut at once but whether he had used the ivy before was what she wanted to know.

Without much hope, Denis pulled aside the leaves, felt down between the stems and suddenly held her breath as her finger touched something hard. A moment later she had scooped it up, wiped off the earth and there it was—the Laurent family ring! Mr. Chip was the thief just as she had hoped he might be when she promised Midge they would find the ring.

Midge would be so happy, was her first thought as she returned the ring to the blue enamel box where it had always been kept. Then she remembered. And suddenly there was a great lump in her throat. Oh, dear, finding the ring now when—— She swallowed desperately and began to prowl about the room again, only to end up before the portrait of Denis Laurent. She could not see him until she had rubbed the mist out of her eyes and then she had the oddest impression that he was smiling sympathetic understanding down at her, just as he had once understood about the kitten.

"Oh, Grandfather," Denis begged silently, "tell me what to do? Where to look?"

She did not hear Nicolette bound away and was still gazing

beseechingly up at the portrait when Angelica's voice startled her.

"You would think Grandfather himself was somewhere behind that painting, wouldn't you?" said Angie in her silkiest tones. "Only he isn't. Jarret and I searched the chimney one summer but all we found was enough soot to get us into real trouble. There's no secret room or anything of the kind."

As Denis turned in time to see her limp to a chair, Angelica added, waving her bandaged foot, "You don't have to look as though I was some kind of spectre. I sprained my ankle, that's all. And if I couldn't skate and dance there was no point in staying so I came home on the early morning train. Where is everybody?"

When Denis did not reply it was Angie's turn to stare. "Dee! Something has happened. What is it?"

Denis swallowed and glanced instinctively at the portrait whereupon the younger girl started up in alarm. *"Bon Dieu!* Not Grandfather?"

"It's—Midge," Denis managed to explain at last. "We can't find her."

"You mean she's lost? Lost! But how? Where?" Angie urged impatiently, her face suddenly the color of the bandage on her ankle.

"We don't—know."

Midge had gone out sometime the afternoon before, Denis explained, and she had not returned. They had hunted all night, Clem and Uncle Guy and the two Dulacs. They were out again now.

"Jeanpierre and his father are with Clem in the woods. Aunt Felice and Uncle Guy have gone in the car and Claire is on horseback, searching some unused road. Angie! Could one of the habitants have kidnapped her?"

Angelica shook an emphatic head. "No. But I wonder——Oh, Dee," she moaned tragically, "I wonder——"

"Wonder what? Angie, you don't mean to say you have any notion of where—— Angie, speak!"

But Angelica could not seem to speak. Denis had to give

her an exasperated shake before she finally admitted that the day before while she was packing the yellow dress, just before they took her to the train, Midge had come into her room wanting to know if she had seen the chipmunk.

"I didn't think she would believe me. Truly I didn't. It was supposed to be a joke."

"What did you tell her?" Denis demanded fiercely.

"I—said it must have been her chipmunk we had seen when we drove past old Bateese Joulin's place on the short cut from school."

"Angie!"

"But I didn't dream—— Oh, Dee! You don't think she believed it?" All Angelica's cool poise was gone.

"I just wonder why they named you after an angel," Denis told her fiercely. "Joulin," she repeated. "Clem said Midge would not be anywhere near old Joulin's place because she was afraid of the old man."

"Yes, I know. He's harmless but Midge once saw old Bateese whip his horse and he only laughed when she cried about it. Do you mean they—haven't—searched that road?" Angie stammered.

But Denis was already on her way to the hall closet and her coat.

Angelica limped after her. "I'm going, too," she announced.

"Don't be absurd," Denis snapped. "You can't walk. Besides, someone has to stay here and answer the telephone. Where can my scarf be?"

"Take mine. And you had better take this heavy sweater of Clem's. And an extra scarf," Angie urged, plying her with warm garments in an effort to help but so frightened she was scarcely conscious of what she said or did.

"Oh, Dee, if anything has happened to her—— Here, wear my red hood. Please, Dee, she could see you easier in case——" Angelica broke off to kneel beside her suitcase, which was still in the hall, and rummage frantically through it.

"Tell me exactly how to get to Joulin's place, Angie," Denis ordered as she tied the crimson hood under her chin,

flung the extra scarf over her shoulders and grabbed the
heavy sweater. Angelica, who had pulled a box of candy out
of the bag and torn off its wrappings, was stuffing chocolates
into her coat pocket.

"Quick," Denis urged. "How do I get there?"

She must go up the road toward the Dulac place, Angie explained. But instead of going on to the Birch Lake path and
the Dulacs' she must turn off at the fork and in about half a
mile she would come to another road.

"Turn west up it and the first house you come to will be
old Joulin's. It's not far from the turn," Angie called from
the door as Denis started off.

Outside it was not as bleak as it looked but there was certainly a feel of snow in the air. Even Denis was aware of it
and in any case she had seen Clem's anxious glance at the
sky when he started off again after drinking some hot coffee.
He had brushed aside her suggestion that perhaps, like Jarret,
Midge had run away. Leave Mr. Chip and her other animals?
Never would Midge do that. And then he had tried to comfort Denis by pointing out that Midge was too familiar with
the woods to lose her head or be afraid.

"But—all night—and she was just over a cold," Denis had
moaned.

Clem said Midge could have survived the night because she
was wise enough to have found some sort of protection. But
if it snowed before they found her——

He hurried off, leaving Denis to listen for the telephone,
visit a tearful Curly Rose in the kitchen and wander miserably
about the living room wondering, in spite of Clem's assur-
ance, whether Midge had gone to look for Jarret. Then she
found the ring and that only made her feel worse. Then Angie
had come.

It was uphill as far as the fork but after that Denis found
herself on a twisting but fairly level dirt road, so that she could
walk faster. But not fast enough. How far was half a mile?
She passed no house and the road seemed interminable, but
finally it ended, running into a poorer road that crossed it at

right angles. Now she had only to go west up this road and the Joulin place was not far. But which way was west?

Denis stood still in dismay. Clem had been trying to teach her how to judge direction by the sun, but this morning there was no sun. Like a dog who has lost the scent she stood bewildered, looking frantically first in one direction and then in the other. One way she could see nothing but woods. In the opposite direction she caught a glimpse of some sort of building up the hill between the trees. That must be the way, because Angie had said to go west *up* the road.

On the scent again, Denis started off eagerly. But when she reached the building she had glimpsed between the trees, it turned out to be a roadside chapel, closed up tight and apparently no longer used. The Joulin place must be around the bend. As she turned to hurry on, something across the road from the deserted chapel caught her eye, a bit of bright blue sticking to one of the bare bushes. Her heart seemed to stop beating. Was it—— Denis pushed her way through to the bush on which it had caught and found no mirage but actually the tassel from Midge's blue cap.

"Midge! Midge!" Denis called and when there was no answer, looked about helplessly. Beyond the tangle of bushes she discovered that the ground sloped steeply to a brook and a wide ravine. Had Midge gone down there?

While Denis hesitated something cold and damp touched her cheek—the first snowflake. In a panic then, she shouted wildly again and again, "Midge! Midge!"

No sound! And now she was looking through a thin veil of snow as more flakes began to drift down. But she must find Midge before the snow made it impossible. She must. Denis walked down a few steps until she could see more of the ravine and the brook and as she did so her foot hit something, something that rolled and bounded down over the hard ground, landing just short of the brook.

As her eyes followed it Denis fairly held her breath and less than a minute after the thing landed had stumbled and slid to it. She gathered up one of the red and white peppermint balls Midge always carried in her pocket and then, across the brook on a grey stone, she saw another. In three leaps she was beside it looking about for more. But either the peppermint balls had given out or——

Denis pulled off her woolly gloves, cupped her hands and shouted as loud as she could down the ravine. When there was no audible response she tried again in the other direction, her voice muted by the thickening white veil all around her. And the silence of the falling snow was frightening. She was gathering the voice and courage to call again when—— Did she imagine it, the faint, ghostly whistle that seemed to come from the edge of the woods, where the trees were vague shapes through the snow? Just ahead, as she moved toward them, was a great pine, its thick branches sweeping the ground.

Under such a pine one could be safe in a snowstorm, Midge had told her only the other day. There would be a little hollow around the tree trunk and the snow outside would act as a protection from the cold. But what matter that the tree was a refuge if she could not find Midge. Desperately Denis shouted once more as she stood beside the pine and had scarcely done so when the low branches moved, parted and revealed—a blue cap.

"Midge! Midge!" She was down on the ground hugging the shivering child close in her arms, hugging her closer when Midge explained through chattering teeth, "I couldn't f—find Mr. Ch—Chip."

The chipmunk was safe at *Manoir Laurent*, Denis told her. "But Angie s—said——"

It was all a mistake, Denis assured her hastily and now they must get home. When she started toward the brook, however, it was no longer there; the veil of snow had become a heavy curtain and only the nearby pine was a recognizable outline. In spite of Midge's protest that she could find the brook, Denis drew the cold child back to the shelter of the tree, rubbed the warmth into her and then fed her some of Angie's chocolates while she hugged her close under Clem's heavy sweater. Somewhere, by the brook no doubt, she had lost the extra scarf.

There was a pile of dry leaves under the pine and before she fell asleep Midge explained that she had spent the night there. She had gone up the road to Bateese Joulin's place yesterday afternoon hunting for Mr. Chip and was still looking when old Bateese came home. He asked what she wanted and just laughed in a scary way when she told him about the chipmunk. Then he pointed down the road and told her to hurry and to be sure and say her prayers. So she had run all the way until she came to the chapel. Mr. Chip wasn't there but she did kneel down and say a prayer.

When she stood up and opened her eyes something moved in the bushes across the road and she scrambled through. But it was only a red squirrel who bounded ahead of her down to the brook. Perhaps Mr. Chip had gone down to the water for a drink, too. She was crying by that time and there wasn't a handkerchief in her pocket, only some peppermint balls, but she ran down to the brook crying and calling. It was almost dusk as she called and called. And then all at once it was so dark she was afraid to go back for fear she would meet old Bateese. She sat on a stone and ate a peppermint and then she saw the great pine and decided to stay under it all night. Perhaps in the early morning she would find Mr. Chip.

So she gathered dry leaves and after a long time fell asleep. When she woke up she was very cold and crawled out to run about and get warm. But outside the pine it was as black as charcoal, no stars, nothing, so she had to go back and huddle into the leaves again. She was so cold she could not go to sleep but finally she must have slept because the next thing she knew someone was calling and she tried to blow on the little whistle Jarret made for her last summer, the day he said he wanted to—— Midge suddenly put a hand over her mouth. Then she said she scarcely could blow the whistle.

"I was so—cold but it's—warmer—n—ow," she murmured sleepily.

Her eyes closed while Denis held her close and tried to

think clearly and without getting into a panic. If Clem or Uncle Guy went home, Angie would tell them she had gone to Joulin's place. But even if they happened to stop at the deserted chapel they would not see the blue tassel because it would be white by now.

The snow was falling so quietly, not blowing, just gently but inevitably covering the ground. And it might go on and on; storms lasted for days in this country she had heard Uncle Guy say. Denis was not cold but she shivered and knew they must stay in the safe nook under the pine. What had Jarret told Midge the day he made the whistle, she wondered, her eyelids drooping wearily. After being up most of last night she wanted only to curl down in the leaves with Midge for a few minutes and forget their predicament.

But she must not fall asleep. That was the one thing she must not do. Denis suddenly laid Midge down and crawled out far enough to gather up a handful of snow and rub it over her face hard. She could think of pleasanter ways to wake up but it served the purpose and now she was able to see more clearly through the thick white veil. And if it was not snowing quite so hard she might find the brook or if she waited a little longer it might stop. While Denis anxiously considered the possibility, she seemed to hear a sound, like a muffled shout from far away. Did she only wish for it? No, there it was again.

In frantic haste, then, she backed under the pine, found the little whistle in Midge's coat pocket and crawled out until she could stand up and blow on it, again and again and again. But when she paused to listen for a response there was nothing but the silent, falling snow. She gave one last despairing blow and as though in answer a dark bulk took shape through the snow curtain. Clem's voice hailed her.

He had the missing scarf in his hand. It had caught on one of the bushes near the road and the snow had not entirely covered it; the bright red against white was like a beacon. But he never would have found them if she had fallen asleep and not heard his shout and blown the little whistle that guided him straight to the pine.

Clem seemed to be able to smell the brook, for once he had Midge in his arms he told Denis to follow; and there it was. Then they were climbing up the slippery bank, pushing through the bushes and out on the road at last, where Clem shouted for Jeanpierre. He had brought the truck as far as the turn into Joulin's road and soon they were driving home, or rather creeping because the snow gathered so quickly on the windshield Clem had to find his way by instinct rather than by sight. It was only then that Denis learned how he actually found her.

At the chapel, the first thing he saw was a patch of red against the white snow where her scarf caught on a branch as she plunged through the bushes. And then his shouts brought the answering whistle.

"You see I made Angie repeat exactly the directions she had given you. So at the road to Joulin's I turned east and——"

"Turned west, you mean," Denis interrupted wearily.

Clem chuckled. "Turned east. Angie told you to go west up the road, didn't she? So I knew you'd just naturally take the wrong direction."

CHAPTER XIII

Denis in Charge

THE SNOW that had started with a few lazy flakes continued to fall all day and night and all the next day, while the temperature dropped steadily. The second morning after Midge was found Denis awoke to see her window framing a world half buried in snow. She stretched, sat up and immediately burrowed back under the down quilts to escape the stinging cold air. She would certainly need a fire this morning, once she had collected enough courage to close the window and light one.

Then she saw the clock and shot up again. Twenty minutes after eight! And no one had wakened her.

"Yes, come in," she called when there was a knock on the door. "How could you let me oversleep, Claire? Aunt Felice will be——"

But it was Angelica. She had on a coat and hat and her face was solemn as she limped in, the ankle still bandaged, and explained that Claire was sick in bed with tonsillitis or something.

"Goodness, it's cold in here, Dee. Stay where you are, I'll close the window and light your fire."

While Denis willingly huddled back under quilts, Angie touched a match to the fire and waited until it blazed up. Then she walked over and stood beside the bed.

"Clem is taking me to the train. Mamma won't let me stay to take care of Midge. It's my punishment," Angelica added tragically. "Dee, will you—write. Just to say how she is every day. Please, Dee."

"Of course I will. And the danger of pneumonia is past, Midge is going to be fine. The doctor said so."

"Yes, I know. But all that snow. Suppose you hadn't found

her when you did?" Angelica shuddered dramatically before she begged again, "Just a card, Dee, each day."

Poor Angie! As punishment for what she had led Midge to believe, Angelica had not been allowed even to see her sister. She had limped unhappily about the house for two days, scarcely eating, and doing anything she was asked to do without complaint. When her mother told her sternly that implying a lie was worse than telling one, she had listened with a white face and then promised that she never would tell even the tiniest little fib again, never.

Whereupon Aunt Felice said impatiently that there were times when it was right and kind to fib, as Angelica ought to know by now. It was time she grew up.

Yes, Angie had certainly suffered for her teasing remark, thought Denis as she dressed. Her fingers were so stiff she had difficulty with the buttons and zippers but twice, in spite of the cold, she was drawn irresistibly to the window.

The country was like a Christmas card. An occasional spruce showed green patches under its cottony trim, here and there a fence post rose dark above the white, but for the most part the fields, the fences and the trees were buried in deep snow. How could Clem drive the car? Then she heard the tinkle of sleigh bells and saw that the road had already been plowed. There they went, half buried in fur rugs, the bells jingling as the horse trotted down the road. Uncle Guy, who was going to Quebec for a few days, was with them. Oh, why hadn't she been up in time to go along? She never had ridden in a sleigh.

Denis said something of the kind to Aunt Felice as soon as she got downstairs. But the older woman only gave her a wan look and remarked dryly that she would have opportunity enough from now on through the winter.

"If you wish something to eat, Denise, you must find it in the kitchen," added Aunt Felice and disappeared with the last of the breakfast dishes. She sounded less annoyed than bewildered, which was so unusual that Denis trailed her in puzzled distress.

In the kitchen everything was in confusion and Curly Rose was crying into the dishwater; her father was very ill, perhaps dying, and she had been sent for. Jeanpierre was getting ready to drive her home. Meanwhile, Aunt Felice told her to go upstairs and pack her bag.

"Denise and I will finish the dishes," said the older woman.

But Aunt Felice did not sound like her usual capable self. She picked up a platter only to put it down aimlessly, and was looking about as though wondering where to start, when the doctor came. She went upstairs with him and Denis tackled the dishes. She had almost finished when they came back.

"Don't worry any more about Midge," the doctor said confidently as he put on his coat. "Keep her quiet another day and she'll be out looking for a wolf to tame. Claire has laryngitis but if she stays in bed and follows orders she will feel a lot better tomorrow. You don't look up to much yourself," he added, eying Aunt Felice shrewdly. "What's the matter?"

"It is nothing. A headache only."

"A sick headache, eh? Take one of those pills I gave you last summer and go to bed."

Aunt Felice shook her head. Bed was impossible. With Claire sick and Curly Rose gone, there was no one to cook or—— Her voice faded off and she pressed a hand to her forehead with a dazed expression.

"Rubbish! You look positively green. Go straight up to bed and stay there. This young lady can take over. Can't you?" he demanded abruptly, turning to Denis.

"Why, yes I—— Of course I can."

"But the bread!" protested the older woman. "It rises now. It must be baked."

"I'll bake it," Denis offered quickly. "I baked the rolls and I've watched Claire handle the bread."

"Certainly. Any idiot can bake a few loaves of bread," said the doctor. "To bed with you. I want to see you upstairs before I leave."

He drove off finally, the tinkle of his sleigh bells grew

fainter and a great hush seemed to envelop the old manor house. Even the dogs and Mr. Chip were up with Midge. The grey Persian, curled up asleep in the sun, looked merely the muff for which she was named, and only the purr of the living room fire broke the quiet.

"You might as well be alone in the house," the portrait of Denis Laurent seemed to say. "What are you going to do first?"

This was certainly her opportunity to hunt out that mysterious song Jeanpierre claimed he didn't know. And she would like to look at the snapshot of Jarret in the Chopin *Étude* book again. It might, it just might, offer a clue as to what Jarret had said to Midge that the child would not tell. But first she must run up and see if Midge and Claire needed anything, then get the bread into the oven.

When she had put fresh wood on the fire in Claire's room, started a jigsaw puzzle for Midge and stopped to pull the curtains for Aunt Felice against the snow glare, Denis went down to the kitchen. There was a chicken on the table and Clem was just going out the door.

"I've got to get back to a sick calf," he called. "The chicken's cleaned. All you have to do is stuff and roast it."

The door closed after him and Denis stared at the chicken. All she knew about roast chicken was eating it. Her mother never had time to more than broil a chop or steak and when they had any roast meat it was in a restaurant. Roasting meant cooking in the oven, but how did one stuff the creature?

While the bread was baking she found a cook book, read all the recipes for poultry stuffing and selected the one that sounded best. It called for stale bread crumbs browned in butter, and Denis could not help thinking that she was fortunate to be at *Manoir Laurent* because at home there never was that much extra butter in the house.

By the time the bread was out of the oven and the chicken in, the sink was full of dishes again and Denis, tantalized by the odor of habitant pea soup that Curly Rose had left simmering in a great kettle on the back of the stove, was hungry.

However, she washed the cooking dishes and peeled some potatoes before she sat down to eat a crust of fresh bread spread with sweet butter and to read the cook book for a surprise dessert. She was assembling the ingredients to make an angel cake when Clem came in.

"I need some hot water. Chicken isn't burning, is it?" he added, sniffing suspiciously.

Denis glanced at the clock. "I shouldn't think so. It has only been in forty-five minutes and the book says to bake for two hours or more."

"Howling cat! But haven't you looked at it?" Clem demanded and promptly opened the oven door. Whereupon his mouth also opened. "Wh—at's that?" he managed finally between whoops of laughter, pointing to the tin cup that stood in the pan beside the chicken.

"The book said to put a cup of water in the pan," Denis informed him with dignity. "Don't you know anything about cooking?"

Clem collapsed onto the nearest chair fairly doubled up with mirth, until Denis shut the oven door. He jumped up then, grabbed a couple of pot holders and lifted the roaster out where he could pour her cup of water into the pan.

"Water, added to the chicken fat, makes the liquid you baste with," he pointed out between chuckles. But when Denis turned aside to hide a very red face, Clem choked back a last snicker and said that actually it was a wonder anyone ever learned anything out of a cook book; a crossword puzzle made more sense any day.

"What are you making there?" he asked, looking over her shoulder. "Angel cake? Howling Cat!"

"It's a surprise for Midge," Denis said stiffly.

"Surprise, eh?" Clem hesitated before he said quickly, "Want some advice? For free? Try angel cake someday when you don't want to surprise anyone but yourself."

He went back to his sick calf and Denis decided to follow his advice, partly because she no longer trusted the cook book. Besides, she must not give him more mistakes to crow over;

never would he forget that cup of water in the roasting pan.

Before the chicken was done and the vegetables cooked, she knew she had been wise not to attempt the angel cake. The morning was gone. And when she had fed the invalids, replenished the fires upstairs and washed the dishes again, the afternoon was half over. She had not even dusted yet and she did want to hunt for that song.

Denis put a log on the fire and moved about the living room with her duster until she reached the piano, where the photograph of Jarret reminded her of the snapshot and she paused to get out the Chopin *Études*. But there was no snapshot in it. Puzzled, she looked through the other Chopin selections and the music bench itself before she decided that the picture was gone.

But where was it? Had Claire put it in a safer place? Had Angelica or Midge taken it? Denis flopped down in the nearest chair to ponder the disappearance of the snap, remembering that Midge had been reluctant to give it up. Why? Was there something about it that might reveal where Jarret was? But how could there be? As she recalled the picture it was a winter scene with Jarret in the foreground. Was there something revealing in the background?

With a mystified shake of the head she got up finally, pushed the chair in which she had been sitting nearer to the adjacent table and immediately stumbled over some object. With a startled exclamation Denis saw that it was a pocket-knife. Why, it was the knife that had fallen out of Jarret's suit.

What was it doing under the chair? Although the chintz valance was deep enough to conceal it, the knife simply could not have been there for any length of time, not in the house of such a meticulous housekeeper as Aunt Felice? Where then, had it come from?

In spite of Clem's accusation that she was seeing Jean-pierre behind every tree, to Denis there was but one answer. Because of Midge, she had not even thought of the knife since Friday morning but now she remembered what she had said to Clem out in the barn, and that Jeanpierre had certainly heard. That he should take the knife only to return it, however, was almost as puzzling as his refusal to recognize the melody she had actually heard him whistle. Why? Why?

Hastily Denis finished dusting, anxious to start a search for the song Jeanpierre claimed he did not know. But she had no sooner opened the music cabinet than she heard the tinkle of sleigh bells and a few minutes later Bruce Walker rang the front doorbell.

He had come to take Claire for a sleigh ride, he announced, as though it was a foregone conclusion she would want to go. When Denis informed him that Claire was sick in bed and could not speak above a whisper he looked annoyed, then glanced into the living room and asked if he could have a drink of water. And could he write Claire a note? Denis, who privately shared Clem's dislike and had no intention of entertaining Bruce Walker, showed him politely into Uncle Guy's office to write his note while she got the water.

When he had gone she ran upstairs with the note, found all three patients asleep and went back down to the music cabinet and her search for the evasive song. But as she handled her grandfather's music, Denis paused more and more frequently to read his marginal notes on selections familiar to her or movements over which she had labored. Occasionally she found notes added or changed and whether he actually played them or only made the corrections for his own interest, the changes were interesting. There were many Canadian songs scattered through the other music but she was still hunting for the one Jeanpierre denied knowing when again she heard the tinkle of sleigh bells coming nearer and nearer.

Whoever it was must have tied his horse beside the woodshed for she saw him walk out toward the barn, but the light was fading so fast Denis could not see who it was. In any case, apparently he was not coming to the house. But it must be time to take tea up to Claire as well as something to Midge.

She switched on a lamp or two before she left the living

room and went out to the kitchen where she made some hot chocolate for Midge and a few jelly sandwiches, as well as tea and toast for Claire, taking her tray upstairs the back way. When she came down the front stairs half an hour later it was dark outside and the only light in the hall came from the living room lamps. Part way down Denis was conscious of a draft and then there was a click, as though the front door had just closed. Nicolette, who was with her, suddenly barked, then dashed on ahead, sniffing along the hall rug to the front door.

Denis could not see the door clearly and anyway, how could it close when it had not been open? Just the same, her heart was thumping as she followed Nicolette, put her tray on a hall chair and opened the door to peer out.

There was no one in sight. Nothing but snow. The gallery had been cleared, however, and a path shovelled from one end out to the road that led past the kitchens to the barn. Nicolette raced straight out to the path barking wildly, but all Denis could see was the indistinct outline of a horse and sleigh as Clem's visitor drove briskly off down the road. The crunch of his runners on the snow and the jingle of his horse's bells, so clear at first, soon faded into the distance. When they were but a ghostly tinkle, the poodle came back and Denis shut the door. She had probably imagined the draft and the click.

All the same she would be glad when Clem came in; the living room looked suddenly full of shadows, unfamiliar and lonely. Not so long ago she was alone much of the time but now it seemed strange and unpleasant. When I get married, thought Denis, I'll have six children—or maybe seven. Concert pianists didn't get married though, did they? Then she would have seven dogs. All poodles, Denis told Nicolette affectionately as she picked up her tray and proceeded to the kitchen where she found Clem, relieved because his calf was going to recover, making coffee.

He said his visitor was old Jules Dulac whose dog was still missing. "And he wanted Grandfather's address."

"I had a visitor, too," said Denis, and smiled at Clem's disgusted expression when she told who it was.

"How about making a chicken sandwich to go with this coffee," he proposed. "I'm starved."

Denis, who felt suddenly like a chicken sandwich herself, started for the pantry only to pause and turn as she remembered her news.

"What do you think I found under a chair in the living room?" she demanded.

"One of Charcoal's bones."

Denis shook her head. "Jarret's pocketknife!"

"Probably been there all the time," said Clem.

"In Aunt Felice's house? Don't be absurd," Denis told him before she went into the pantry.

She came out immediately, sputtering. "Chicken sandwich indeed! When you've already eaten most of it."

"I haven't touched the chicken since noon," said Clem in such obvious surprise that it was impossible not to believe him.

"But who has then? When I put it away there was one whole side untouched. Now, as you can see, there's nothing but carcass and a little stuffing. Who ate it?"

"Someone who didn't have sense enough to appreciate the stuffing," Clem said, grinning. "Bruce Walker probably."

"Impossible! How could——" Denis stopped, remembering that she had left Bruce Walker in Uncle Guy's office and that from there it was possible to go through the dining room to the pantry without going near the kitchen where she was getting him a glass of water. But if Bruce was as hungry as that he would have said so. And there was the mysterious click of the front door closing, long after Bruce had gone.

"It must have been old Jules," Denis said quickly.

Clem shook his head. "Old Jules wasn't out of my sight, either in the barn or here in the kitchen," he objected.

"Oh!" said Denis. In that case Clem would only laugh at her if she told him about the front door. "Was anyone with old Jules?" she asked suddenly.

"Yes, he had the old fellow with the eye patch along."

"Then his friend must have sneaked into the kitchen while I was upstairs."

But again Clem shook his head. "You had just left as we came in. I saw you pick up the tray as we stepped on the back gallery."

"But somebody ate the chicken," Denis insisted.

"Must have been Bruce Walker," said Clem.

"Don't be ridiculous! Why would Bruce Walker want to steal chicken?

And if she had closed the front door when Bruce left, as she was certain she had, one of the Frenchmen could only have come in through the kitchen, however he went out. Clem must be mistaken.

"I still think it was old Jules or his friend. What did he want anyway?"

"Grandfather's address, I told you. And some information about a stove he wants to buy. Going to Montreal to get it."

"He's going to Montreal?" Denis was suddenly alert. "When?"

"Next week, Tuesday I think he said. How about a ham sandwich, since Bruce ate the chicken? There's almost half a ham in the cold pantry."

Denis made a sandwich for herself as well and by the time she sat down to eat it seemed to have forgotten the perplexing disappearance of the chicken.

"Clem, do you know whether Uncle Guy or anyone has a picture of the old *château* on Hidden Pond? Before it burned, I mean."

"No, I'm afraid it was a ruin before the time of photographs. But somewhere Dad has a book about the old manor houses and *châteaux* of this part of the country and there's a drawing in that, made from descriptions of the place. Why are you so interested? As I remember the drawing of it, the place was not a patch on *Manoir Laurent*. Do you realize that this is one of the finest old houses in the province?"

"I don't know about beauty but there couldn't be a house

to match it for spooks," said Denis, giving the chicken carcass a rueful glance. "Jarret's knife vanishes and as mysteriously reappears. And this afternoon, out of two visitors one scarcely had the time to do it and the other wasn't out of sight, yet half a chicken has been eaten."

In addition, she thought to herself, a snapshot had disappeared and either the front door gave an excellent imitation of closing or both she and Nicolette were crazy.

CHAPTER XIV

Room with Eight Sides

In the living room at *Manoir Laurent* the fire burned with a steady purr, broken by an occasional crackle or sudden hiss, and Denis neglected her book to watch it. She was aglow with a warmth that had nothing to do with fires because Midge, ordered to bed after their fun at the piano, had just given her such a quick, tight hug.

"Thank you for singing, Dee," she had whispered.

Thus Denis watched the upward lick of the flame change from green to purple and stole a contented look around the room. Uncle Guy was reading his paper beside one lamp, Aunt Felice and Claire sat either side of another, knitting, and Clem, in the wing chair opposite, was absorbed in a thick tome. Nicolette's woolly head rested on her shoe. Outside, it was so cold that the trees cracked in the forest; you could hear sounds a long way off and the snow squeaked under your feet. But here, beside the fire, it was—perfect.

She looked up at the portrait of her grandfather, that secretive look of mischief so like Angie's in his black eyes; and he seemed a living part of the group. As the rainbow colors gave way to a yellow flame, Denis had an idea he would agree with her about the fire. But she was unconscious of having spoken until Clem looked up.

"What are you murmuring in your beard?"

Denis started.

"You said something to Grandfather," he prompted.

"Oh! That I like the fire better without that stuff Bruce gave Claire to sprinkle on it. There is something false about all those colors, like—like strawberry ice cream that isn't made of real strawberries."

"Or green carnations," Clem agreed. "Or Bruce himself."

Denis glanced uneasily toward Claire.

"I see you are reading that old book of Dad's," said Clem. "Find the *Château Montagne?*"

Denis merely nodded. She did not want to tell Clem what she had learned about the *château*—not yet.

"Jeanpierre says you made a record today skiing," Clem remarked unexpectedly.

"I had only one spill if that's what he means."

"It means he is pleased with your progress."

"Jeanpierre is a good teacher, very patient," Denis conceded before she settled down to her book.

Uncle Guy had found it for her the day after someone ate the chicken. That perplexing incident remained unsolved, along with the disappearance of two jars of wild strawberry jam from the same pantry. Aunt Felice was particularly annoyed about the jam and half inclined to agree with Clem that Bruce might be the culprit.

"We made so little wild strawberry this year and it is your grandfather's favorite. I had put the two jars away for him," she complained.

Denis, who couldn't believe Bruce Walker responsible for either theft, finally told about the front door. Whereupon Clem laughed at her as she had known he would.

"But I felt a draft and then the door clicked. And Nicolette barked and sniffed about the hall," she insisted.

"Which means nothing because a mouse is a better hunter than Nicolette," said Clem. "She probably sensed that you were startled and decided to give you something to worry about. Moreover, if you shut the door after Bruce, there was no one in the house to go out."

So the disappearance of the chicken and the jam was still a puzzle. Denis felt responsible because she had been in charge of the house and when Claire, better but not really well, croaked in an injured tone that the music was all upset again, she hastily offered to put it in order.

But on opening the cabinet Denis realized that neither her search for the song nor the picture had scattered the music as she found it. It looked as though someone in frantic haste had pawed through the books and sheets. Was he looking for the snapshot of Jarret? Or had Jeanpierre tried to find and remove the song he pretended not to know? He might possibly have been in the house and slipped out the front way when he heard her coming downstairs. But if it was Jeanpierre, why didn't he want her to find that song? Why?

Denis sighed and bent over her book. In it she had already come upon some information about *Château Montagne* that made her impatient for Tuesday and the absence of old Jules. But since the book had been written in a disorderly fashion there was always the possibility of digging out more. And in the very last chapter she found the study of the original owner described as a room unique in French Canada.

"—and from without the square stone walls of *Château Montagne* who would suspect that the count's study, connected with his bedchamber above, had eight sides, that the walls, lined with bookshelves from floor to ceiling were fashioned of seasoned walnut and—"

When Denis closed the book at last her eyes were dark with excitement. Thank goodness she did not have to wait much longer. Tomorrow would be Tuesday, and with Jules Dulac in Montreal, she intended to ski over to the ruin and look for the passage to the tower.

"Why are you so anxious to get into the tower?" the amused black eyes of her grandfather seemed to question as Denis looked up at the portrait.

Because no one had seen it for such a long time, because it was inaccessible, forbidden, would have been her answer had he asked the question in person. But was that the only reason?

"Tuppence for your thoughts," said Clem suddenly.

"They are worth two bits," Denis retorted. She asked quickly, "The skiing will still be good tomorrow, won't it?"

Clem grinned. "Yes, I think you'll be able to practice that turn Jeanpierre showed you."

And although the mercury in the thermometer fell a few

degrees more, so that a glass dish in the corner cupboard broke during the night and you could hear the whistle of the train as far away as Trois Lacs, by noon the sun on the snow was almost hot. Denis started out right after dinner and had to shed her extra sweater before she reached Birch Lake. She was looking for the connection between the lake and Hidden Pond when a voice hailed her and there was Clem, skimming across the snow-covered lake.

"From your expression I gather that I'm about as welcome as a hungry polar bear," he remarked when he had pulled up beside her and was resting on his poles. "What's up?"

Denis made a belated attempt to conceal her exasperation while she surveyed him, at·a loss. Now she must either forget

her attempt to find the secret passage or invite Clem to come along. The trouble was that old Jules might not go away again for a long time, and even if he did, they might have a snow-storm or something to prevent her from trying again. Besides, she was too impatient to wait. She would simply have to take Clem into her confidence and let him laugh if she proved wrong.

"I should think you'd work at this time of day," she grumbled before admitting where she was bound.

Clem looked at Denis, amazed. "But I told you we had already hunted for a passage to the tower. Why, every summer for years Claire and Jarret and I tried to find one. If we failed in mid-summer, how can you find anything with the ruin buried in snow and the temperature twenty below. Or do you expect to shovel off the snow and then move a few tons of stones?" he demanded.

"I don't believe that's where it is," said Denis.

"Oh? And where do you expect to find it?"

"I think maybe—— Oh, come along and I'll show you," she said. "If I'm wrong you can crow."

"And will," Clem warned.

He proposed going up over the hill and around the pond instead of across it since their ski trail would be all too easy to follow that way. But when he saw that there were already ski tracks across Hidden Pond and on the slope, he said they might as well take the short route. Evidently Jules, or more likely Jeanpierre, had already crossed the pond.

"Now what?" Clem demanded when they reached the small wooden house Jules Dulac had built himself against the only remaining portion of the *château*, and had poled around to the front of it. Beyond the house was a shed for his horse, empty now except for an old tom cat who snarled inhospitably at them. Beyond the shed Denis stopped and gazed up at the remaining end of *Château Montagne* against which it was built. This portion, perhaps half a room on each floor, had been rudely walled in with stones and plaster, leaving no windows except those on the pond side.

"What now?" Clem repeated when Denis moved back to the shed. The cat, its eyes shining eerily from a dark corner, snarled an angry protest but ran when she threw a chunk of snow at him.

"What now? Do you expect to find the entrance to a seventeenth century secret passage in a twentieth century shed?" Clem inquired dryly.

"No, but I'd like to get that door in the far corner open. Do you think we could?" said Denis who was already unstrapping her skis.

Clem removed his own, lifted out the wooden peg that held the door closed and pulled it open. "Probably a root cellar, it's black enough. But, enter, Mademoiselle."

Denis had brought her small flashlight and this revealed another door at the foot of two or three steps. Was it locked? No, it opened easily and Denis held her breath while Clem pushed it back.

"The octagonal study!" she announced triumphantly, when the flash showed them, not a root cellar but half of a room, panelled in walnut and lined with shelves from floor to ceiling. Three of the original sides were intact and half of a fourth and fifth. These were joined by the rude wall of plaster and stone they had seen from outside.

Denis explained that she had read about the room in Uncle Guy's book. In some way, presumably by a hidden staircase, it was connected with the bedchamber of the count on the first floor.

"I see now why we had to go down a few steps. The *château* was built on a slope and there was an extra story on the pond side."

"Apparently," Clem agreed. "Only what has it to do with a passage to the tower?"

Denis, who was standing in the middle of the room flashing her light first on one wall and then another, made an impatient sound.

"Only that I've suspected all along it would be the owner who used any secret passage to the tower," she confided.

"And naturally he would want it where he alone had access to it. That's why I wanted to find out whether his rooms were in this end or the other."

"I say, Dee, that was rather bright of you," said Clem. "Do you—— What now?"

For an excited exclamation had escaped Denis as she played her flash up and down the wall to the right of that containing the only window. When she kept it shining on the fourth shelf from the floor, Clem whistled.

"A lantern, by ginger," he exclaimed. "And one that has been recently used."

After that Clem had little difficulty in locating the spring that swung the wall of shelves open, revealing a steep flight of steps leading down to a narrow door. On opening this they were greeted by a damp odor, saw a long sloping tunnel ahead and knew they had found the entrance to the tower.

But Denis' ardor had suddenly cooled. "I suppose there are—are things down there," she murmured with a shudder of distaste.

"Things?"

"Crawling things."

Clem snorted. "Howling Cat! What did you expect? A red velvet carpet and brocade on the walls?"

"N—oo. But it's so—dank." Denis shivered.

"If that isn't like a girl! Crazy to find a way into the tower and now you've found it balk at a little dampness. Or a possible bug! Well, for your comfort, the crawling things are probably hibernating in this weather. So come along."

Since her flash was so small they had better take the lantern as well, Clem suggested, digging into his pocket for a match. Denis vigorously endorsed the proposal and the lantern certainly made the passage less forbidding. No crawling things scuttled from its light but they had to walk bent over and the way seemed interminable before they saw a door ahead. Once through it they were in the tower.

They climbed a winding stone staircase that had no hand rail to a round room with recessed windows less than a foot

in width. Under one of these was an ancient chest, warped and cracking and there was a cot beneath another. Beyond it stood a kind of tall cupboard, its wood stained and cracked. But the plain wooden table and chair in the middle of the room were both new. There was a cracked plate on the table, a soiled cup and saucer and a broken violin bow. For the rest nothing but some yellowed newspapers, dead flies and plenty of cobwebs.

Denis looked so disappointed that Clem demanded, "What did you expect? A sleeping princess? Or the Indian girl's skeleton?" He eyed the cot thoughtfully. "Old Jules probably uses the place in summer, I suppose. It would be cool here on hot nights."

After sniffing at the cup Clem went over to one of the narrow windows. It was the one from which he could see the *château* rather than the pond, and Denis, who had stopped to pick up a piece of paper from under the table, straightened in alarm at his exclamation.

"Howling Cat! Old Jules must be back!"

"Back? How could he be? The Montreal train doesn't get in until after six," Denis objected.

But unfortunately old Jules had not gone to Montreal after all, Clem informed her. According to Jeanpierre, the old man had decided to do his shopping in Quebec. "And see for yourself. That's the smoke of a fresh fire coming out of his chimney."

Denis peered out the narrow slit in the tower wall that served as a window. "Do you think he has had time to find our skis and fasten the door to the passage? So we cannot get out?" she added in dismay.

"Time?" Clem suddenly looked at his watch and shook a relieved head. "No, because he can't even be there. The Quebec train wasn't due at Trois Lacs until twenty minutes ago and it's a good half-hour's drive or more up over the hill from there. He must have arranged for someone to start his fire for him. Look, it's Jeanpierre," Clem added.

A figure on skis appeared around the corner of Dulac's house and shot along the slope with the grace and skill of an expert. They watched him pole up through the woods toward his own house on the other side of the hill before Denis spoke.

"Do you think Jeanpierre saw our skis in the shed?"

"I doubt it. He would have no reason to go into the shed. But if that train was on time we've got to get out of here. And fast."

He started for the stairs while Denis looked regretfully around the room, then hastily gathered up the piece of paper she had noticed under the table, stuffed it into her pocket and followed. The lantern was back on its shelf and they were in the shed, strapping on their skis when they heard the distant tinkle of sleigh bells.

"Will he get here in time to see us ski across the pond?" Denis breathed.

"We'll go by the road. Are you ready? Once around the first bend we won't have to worry."

The road was uphill and Denis had poled so hard she was out of breath by the time they were safely around the bend. But as she sat on a stone to adjust one of her ski straps she panted a question.

"Clem! Are you sure Jarret wasn't interested in music?"

CHAPTER XV

A Cup of Tea

THE WEATHER and the snow continued to be excellent for skiing. Denis, who knew only city snow that each day turned more grey until the streets were fringed with black-coated piles, was surprised every morning to find the world still white.

"The snow at *Manoir Laurent* belongs in a Santa Claus world," she wrote her mother Friday.

Her letter finished, Denis took a small, rumpled piece of paper out of the zipper pocket of her purse and examined it thoughtfully for perhaps the twentieth time. This scrap she had picked up in the tower presented such a tantalizing puzzle. Torn from a grocery store advertisement, on one side it offered hams, bacon, canned tomatoes and soap at bargain prices. But on the other side someone had pencilled several bars of music. And the strange, exciting thing was that they were part of the mysterious air she had heard Jeanpierre whistle.

Clem had already repeated that Jarret was not interested in music. Did the French boy play the piano then? Did old Jules Dulac?

When Clem said that as far as he knew old Jules played only the fiddle, Jeanpierre nothing, and what was it all about? she showed him the paper.

He frowned over the pencilled notes before he shrugged. "I don't know how this got into the tower but it was written by Grandfather. That's the bluish lead of his special pencil, the one Ma Tante claims the crow made off with last June," Clem added with a skeptical grin.

"But Grandfather hasn't been here for nearly a year," Denis protested.

"I know. So this must be quite old. But don't get any crazy notions about Jeanpierre or old Jules, because it was written by Grandfather; the only mystery is how it got into the tower."

That was where he was wrong. Although she did not say so, Denis was more puzzled than ever by the paper. Her grandfather had been away for months and the music had been written with his pencil, stolen in June. Yet the grocery advertisement carried an *August* date.

What did it mean?

That Denis Laurent could not have written the music, for one thing. But who had then? Jeanpierre? Old Jules? Someone who had had an opportunity to steal the pencil certainly. She might find the answer if only she could search that room in the tower. After all, she and Clem had left hurriedly without looking into anything. What did the chest under the window contain? And they had not opened the drawer in the table or looked into the cupboard. She must go back, thought Denis, as she put the paper reluctantly away.

She looked about for the French cook book Aunt Felice had suggested she study, only to remember that she had left it in Midge's room.

In his box, Mr. Chip was curled into a brown ball. He had gone to sleep when the temperature dropped below zero and had not moved since. In fact he was so sound asleep that yesterday Midge had actually rolled him about the box without waking him, and he had had no food for days. It was strange the light did not bother him, thought Denis, and pushed his box over a few inches where it was darker. The change had no effect on Mr. Chip, who remained an inanimate ball of brown fur, but it revealed something under his box, something Denis had been looking for and that she hastened to pick up.

So it was Midge who had taken the picture of Jarret. But why? It was only the snapshot of a boy with a pair of skates slung over his shoulder as he stood beside——

"Dee! Oh, Dee, are you up here?"

Denis hastily slipped the picture into the cook book before she answered, "Yes. What is it?"

"Mamma wants us all in the living room in five minutes," Claire explained. "She has sent for Clem, too."

"What's up?"

Claire shook her head before hurrying on. She did not know but her mother looked *très sérieuse*.

Denis stopped long enough in her own room to get out a magnifying glass and examine the snap of Jarret under it. That stone wall behind him? Was it the tower on Hidden Pond? But why hide a picture because it showed Jarret beside the tower? Why did Midge think the snapshot gave any clue to what Jarret was doing? Perhaps—perhaps Midge knew there was something in the tower that would give Jarret away. Yes, that might be it and the only way to find out was to visit the place again.

After memorizing the picture, Denis slid it back under Mr. Chip's box and went downstairs where she found Uncle Guy, Claire and even Curly Rose with Aunt Felice in the living room.

Clem came in a minute or two later and Aunt Felice, who could be so gracious, surveyed them all coldly. She held up the blue enamel snuff box containing the Laurent family ring and asked sternly, "You are quite sure you put the ring back in this box the morning of the storm?"

With a start of dismay, Denis realized that the question was addressed to her. "Why—yes. Yes, I know I did."

"Have you touched it since?"

Denis could only shake her head in bewilderment.

"Have any of you touched or seen it?" Aunt Felice demanded. "*Non?* Yet your grandfather's ring is not here," she announced, showing them that the box was empty.

Clem whistled softly. "What? With Mr. Chip asleep? And no crow in the house," he muttered.

"It is not an affair for *plaisanterie*," Aunt Felice reproved him. "The Laurent ring has gone. It is possible that Denise was correct about the front door."

"Unless Bruce had a fancy for rings as well as chicken and jam," Clem murmured under his breath.

But Claire heard and gave him an indignant glance.

Denis stared at the empty snuff box, her thoughts in a whirl. Whoever scattered the music must also have stolen the ring. She could not believe Jeanpierre would do that; but what had anyone else expected to find in the music cabinet?

Hazily she heard Uncle Guy suggest that Midge might have removed the ring to what the child considered a safer place; they could question her as soon as she returned from the convent. But Denis thought it most unlikely and her thoughts returned to the room in the tower, to the possibility of finding more clues there. Somehow she was convinced that those bars of music, pencilled on the back of a grocery ad, offered a key to the whole mystery. When Clem came back in for the noonday meal she cornered him.

"You know very well Midge didn't touch the ring. But are you sure about that Jules Dulac. And his friend? Could he have slipped into the house while you were talking to old Jules?"

Clem lounged beside the window and took an exasperating time to light his pipe before he nodded toward the road. "Why not ask Jules himself? There he goes, headed for Laurentville."

Denis replied with a scathing look, but as she watched the sleigh, its driver's fur-capped head just visible above the rugs, go flying past the *Manoir* road, her pulse quickened. The opportunity to pay another visit to the tower had come more quickly than she could have dreamed possible and she would start as soon as she could get away after dinner.

Fortunately Clem went straight into Uncle Guy's office from the dining room, Jeanpierre was chopping wood, and no one noticed that instead of practicing the new ski turn, Denis had gone on to Birch Lake and across Hidden Pond to the ruined *château*. There she found the snow so well packed that she decided to leave her skis under the big spruce on the pond side, where they were less likely to be noticed than in the shed.

This time, with not even a cat to delay her, Denis was soon through the shed door and down in the eight-sided room. She had swung the wall open and was about to step into the passage when she heard a sound. And as she listened the faint, ghostly tinkle became a jingle, the jingle of approaching sleigh bells. Someone passing? No, the sleigh had stopped, a horse neighed; old Jules was back.

Denis hastily swung the wall closed and switched off her light. Better to face him here than be marooned in the tower. And perhaps he would not notice that the peg was out of the door; perhaps he would go on into the house after he had unharnessed. Then she could slip out. Cautiously she felt her way across the room and flattened herself against the wall behind the open study door.

Would he never stop talking to the horse? He spoke so fast Denis could not make out a word, but at last he stopped. She waited to make doubly sure he had gone before moving from behind the door and switching on her flash. Then her heart seemed to be in her throat; she wanted to scream and could not. For the flash lighted a moving wall of shelves and a *hand*, a hand that she knew instantly was not that of Jules Dulac. Her eyes must have closed momentarily, for now the hand was not there. And neither, a moment later, was Denis.

She was in the shed, edging around the wall, past the horse and out where she could draw a long, thankful breath, until she remembered that she could not reach her skis without passing the house. Unless she went all around the ruin and even that way she chanced being seen. She must either leave her skis and walk the road home, or face old Jules. While Denis hesitated, the decision was made, for there he was, coming toward her with feed for his horse.

When he glared at her in astonishment, Denis stammered that she had been skiing. But she was cold, so cold. "*J'ai froid,*" she shivered. It was not hard to shiver under the chilling gaze of the old Frenchman.

"Skis?" he repeated, staring at her feet.

When Denis explained that she had left them under the spruce, old Jules scowled suspiciously, whereupon she shivered again. And this time her shiver was real enough to be convincing apparently because the Frenchman promptly ushered her into his warm house.

It was scarcely the visit Denis had planned but she was relieved not to be caught in the tower passage and so really cold that she stood thankfully over the stove. The room was a kitchen which served also as general living room and proved Clem's contention that most habitant houses, so picturesque outside, had little attraction within. The furnishings were useful but ugly. Denis was looking around idly, her real thoughts on the hand she had seen in the octagonal room, when old Jules suddenly asked whether she would like a cup of tea.

Tea?

Because she did not know what else to do, Denis accepted. "*Mais oui. Merci beaucoup*. Thank you very much."

Smiling inwardly at the thought of Clem's face could he see her drinking tea with old Jules Dulac, she sat down in a hideous but not uncomfortable rocker while her host put a kettle of water on the fire and brought out a pot and some cups. When he went off with a pitcher, presumably for milk, Denis looked absently at the violin hanging on the wall and wondered how she could find out to whom that *hand* belonged. Could it possibly be Jarret's?

"Why you ski alone?" her host demanded abruptly on his return with the milk.

It was such an unexpected question that Denis was still searching for an answer when there was a knock on the door and there was the old man's friend, the crony with the eye patch. Today he wore also a piece of cloth wound high around his neck, over his chin and up around his head under the old felt hat he made no attempt to remove. Evidently this curious bandage was to protect his throat for the hoarse voice in which he greeted them told of a bad cold. He accepted a cup of tea, drank it with obvious relish and then suddenly nodded at the fiddle indicating that he wanted Jules to play.

With obvious reluctance the habitant took down his fiddle and played some of the native airs. When he paused to adjust a string Denis seized the opportunity to hum as much of the mysterious melody as she knew and to ask what song it was.

Old Jules merely shook his head, indicating that he did not know, but his friend urged her to hum it again. Yet when she complied he, too, shook his head. And why did she like that tune? he wanted to know.

Denis said slowly that it made her think of the river, and of wind in the pines, and of Indians and—and church bells.

The man seemed to understand for he croaked a comment. "*L'esprit du pays, eh?* The spirit of French Canada, you think? *Mais oui, c'est ça*. Yes, it is that."

He was sitting in the darkest corner of the room and Denis, who had been watching his hands, suddenly realized that the reason she could not see them very well was that it was almost dusk. She rose in alarm. Whereupon the visitor also rose and remarked that she never would get home before dark now. Jules must drive her back.

Old Jules glowered at him, then shrugged acquiescence and went off to harness the horse while the crony chortled over his discomfiture. He finally croaked a "*bon soir*" to Denis and started down the road in the direction of the hill parish leaving her to climb into Jules Dulac's sleigh and be driven off in the opposite direction.

Although the afternoon had scarcely worked out as planned, long before they pulled up to the front entrance of *Manoir Laurent*, sleigh bells jingling, Denis suspected that she had seen something more important than any object she might have found in the tower. In any case she knew the afternoon was not lost when Clem opened the door and saw her escort.

CHAPTER XVI

An Invitation

"WANT to ski across country to Trois Lacs this afternoon, Dee?" said Clem who was having a mid-morning cup of coffee and a snack in the kitchen.

Denis stirred the habitant pea soup and ladled out a spoonful to taste. Was it the clove of garlic Aunt Felice had told her to add, or the herbs, tarragon and summer savory and parsley, or the quarter cup of wine vinegar that gave such a delicious flavor? Whatever it was, she agreed with Angie, who said her mother's brand of pea soup was like a sparrow transformed into a nightingale.

"I can't," Denis murmured.

"Why can't you?" said Clem. "And what about another sugar bun?"

Denis brought him one, watched anxiously as he bit into it and admitted that the buns were her product.

"So that's what is wrong with them," said Clem, then grinned at her crestfallen look, finished off the bun, smacked his lips and remarked, "You know, I shouldn't be surprised if you turned out to be a pretty good cook. You really like to cook, don't you?"

Denis nodded enthusiastically. "Aunt Felice makes it seem important, like painting a picture or—or composing a song. And there are such good things to work with."

"We do have good eats on the farm, from dairy products and Dulac's garden vegetables to the fish and game. And Ma Tante certainly knows what to do with food," Clem agreed. He put down his empty coffee cup and added slyly, "Moreover, you have watched old Jules make tea. That should be an education. Tea, indeed!"

"Whatever do you mean?" Denis demanded.

"Just that I wonder the old man had any in the house. Coffee or chocolate, yes, but not tea. Well, now you have sipped tea with him are you convinced that old Jules had nothing to do with the disappearance of the ring?"

"No—oo. I still think his friend might——"

"Bosh," Clem interrupted. "Put that notion out of your head. Why can't you ski to Trois Lacs? Afraid of the distance?"

"Claire and Bruce have invited me to drive to Laporte and watch a habitant skating contest."

"And you are going?" Clem demanded scornfully. "That Bruce Walker! Always urging more habitants to go into the textile mills, when they belong on the soil or in the woods. It's bad. They understand the earth and love it, but coax them into the mills and they'll lose all their zest for life."

Clem added with a snort of impatience, "Why Claire bothers with that Walker fellow I don't understand. Can't you tell her he's no good?"

"Oh, Clem! That would only make her stick up for him. You just have a hate on the man. You're as bad as Angie."

Clem growled as he put on his leather jacket, "He is not good enough for Claire. But that's right; Angie has no use for him either. Maybe——" He stopped. "Well, have a good time playing chaperone," he said disagreeably and slammed the door as he went out.

Denis watched him from the kitchen window while she ate one of the sugar buns herself. She was proud of them and thrilled about all the things she had learned to make during the past few weeks. It was exciting to produce a meat pasty or a fruit tart that tempted Uncle Guy to ask for a second or third helping. Hours spent in the kitchen seemed to fly. In fact the days passed all too quickly. It was over a week since her visit to the ruin that had ended in such a strange tea party, and Christmas was less than three weeks away. Denis had realized it suddenly yesterday when Aunt Felice started to make the first fruit cakes.

As Clem disappeared into the barn, Denis wondered what

he had started to say about Angie. She was not surprised that the mention of Bruce Walker had annoyed him because it always did. Worse, he would stalk rudely out of the room after a curt greeting whenever Bruce came to the house. He insisted the man was too old for Claire, that he had eaten the chicken and was no good anyway.

Denis did not like Bruce Walker either, but it was preposterous to think he had eaten that chicken or stolen jam

and a ring. Well, perhaps the jam. But nothing else. And Clem was so prejudiced. His attitude did not help. But why had he mentioned Angie and then stopped?

Denis wondered again as she sat behind Bruce and Claire in the sleigh that afternoon. From her nest of furs she could see Bruce's shoulders and the back of his fur-capped head, but of Claire only her blue hood, lined and edged with beaver. Because one's ears must be protected against the sub-zero cold

she could not hear what the two in front were saying, but she knew by the way the blue hood turned to laugh up at the fur cap that they were absorbed in each other.

Could it be possible Clem was jealous? He treated Claire like a sister of whom he was particularly fond, yet actually he was no relation to her. Denis found the thought that he might be jealous of Bruce so unaccountably disturbing that she thrust it aside. Fortunately she had other things to ponder as they flew over the snow-packed road, their sleigh bells jingling.

Clem's remark about Jules Dulac making tea had turned her thoughts back to the unexpected visit with the old man and his friend. She saw again the *hand*, as it rested on a moving wall of shelves, she recalled the hand of Dulac's crony. And her memory returned to the rainy afternoon when Jarret had sat beside her in the train, his hand resting on a small paper package while he confided his intention of running away. There was something so very like about those three hands that Denis was haunted by them. Yet their very likeness was mystifying.

Suddenly aware that Claire had turned and was trying to make her hear, Denis lifted her hood.

"Are you warm enough? That's Laporte, between the hills to the north," Claire added.

Still uncertain about points of the compass, Denis looked the wrong way before she saw it across the valley, a few houses huddled about a tall, silvery church steeple. The village was two miles away, however, and by the time they got there the contests had started. Spectators in colorful jackets and caps, shouting encouragement or disapproval, made a gay scene of it. Denis was always fascinated at the habitant rinks by the bright colors and the laughter and the songs. Today there was someone with a mouth organ. And a fire had been built nearby where the onlookers retired to warm themselves from time to time or to argue about the respective merits of a favored contestant.

By the time they arrived the second contest was over; the

winner had removed his skates and was standing with the rest of the contestants jabbering in French. When, as the others returned to the ice for the next number, he walked off jauntily, his skates slung over his shoulder, Denis's eyes followed him in startled excitement. She never had seen the young habitant before and probably never would again, but unexpectedly he had supplied the answer to a puzzle.

She knew now why Midge had hidden the snapshot of Jarret and the reason was so obvious that she felt stupid not to have seen it long ago. It explained the ticket to Trois Lacs perhaps and even, possibly, the hand she had seen in the octagonal room. Suddenly Denis knew, or thought she did, why Jarret had run away. But if she had guessed correctly she knew also that she no longer wanted to find him—not yet.

Preoccupied by her discovery and its implications, Denis was unaware that the next contest had started until Bruce drew her attention to one of the skaters. Claire had walked away to speak with a young Frenchwoman she knew.

"There is the boy I saw last week," Bruce pointed out. "He's young but his spins are worth watching and he has some new figures. See him? The skinny boy in brown?"

Denis nodded impatiently, her eager attention on the boy in question as he executed a difficult figure with skill and grace, then drew off to the opposite side of the rink while another contestant tried the same figure and brought a "Boo!" from the audience. He was the same boy she had noticed that day with Clem, the boy who reminded her of Jeanpierre.

"That's the boy I told you about, who created a sensation in Quebec," Bruce was saying to Claire. "Nobody seems to know anything about him except that he has a long French name. Comes from one of the hill parishes, I believe. There goes the last contestant for this number and the boy was better than any of them. I'm going around and see if I can talk to him when he comes off."

But by the time Bruce reached the other side of the rink the boy in brown had disappeared and nobody seemed to know what had become of him. On the other hand no one seemed surprised.

"I talked to a couple of the older men and they tell me the boy always disappears after he wins a contest. Doesn't like a fuss made over him." Bruce Walker shrugged. "Good publicity, if you ask me. And a kid as clever as that probably knows it."

"Or he could be shy," said Claire.

"Not he," Bruce scoffed. "Making a mystery of himself is a clever stunt."

Denis, too, would have liked to see the boy closer and she was disappointed when he did not appear again. But she had more than the skater to think about on the way home. Nestled deep into her rugs in the back seat of the sleigh, she was so quiet that Claire thought she had fallen asleep.

Actually her mind was busy with the problem of Jarret. Midge knew only that her cousin wanted to be a skater; she hid the snapshot fearing it would give him away. But if Jarret had run away because he wanted to be a professional skater and was hiding in the ruin, the hand on the moving wall of shelves was explained. Or was it? Jarret might know of a way to get into *Manoir Laurent;* he could have eaten the chicken and upset the music cabinet looking for the snapshot. But would he have stolen his grandfather's ring? Even if he had no other way of bribing old Jules to hide him? Surely he would have taken something with money value only. And what about the melody of Hidden Pond, the bit of music she had found in the tower?

When they reached home at last Denis was still trying to solve the puzzle. She warmed her hands at the living room fire wondering why the things she knew didn't quite fit together.

"Contests worth it?" Clem demanded curtly by way of greeting.

Worth the trip with Bruce Walker, was what he meant but Denis was not paying attention. She was gazing thoughtfully at the portrait of her grandfather in whose laughing black eyes she sensed much wisdom.

Uncle Guy smiled at her absorption. "There was a letter from Father today. He is in London now and won't be home for Christmas. But he has sent something for each of us."

Denis turned suddenly. "For Christmas? Did you say Grandfather would be home for Christmas?"

Clem scowled at her. "Dad said he would *not* be home. What's the matter? Did the sleigh ride with Bruce freeze your ears?" he demanded sourly.

Denis only smiled pleasantly at him. It would have been nice to have her grandfather for Christmas but the important thing was that again he had come to the rescue, added a vital bit of information to what she already had. She did not know yet how it would solve her puzzle but she smiled peacefully at Clem and chortled inwardly over her discovery.

CHAPTER XVII

Christmas Eve

DENIS put another stick of wood into the stove, set the dampers and slid her mince pie carefully into the oven. While it baked she wandered into the living room, deserted except for Nicolette, and stood thoughtfully gazing up at the portrait of Denis Laurent. His Christmas packages had come yesterday, including a box for her, a box with a Paris label. She could scarcely wait to see what it contained.

She turned presently and surveyed the room with satisfaction. It looked so Christmasy, decorated with the greens they had gathered. And the tree was set up, ready to be trimmed tonight. Idly Denis strolled over to the piano.

> "It came up—on the midnight clear,
>   That glo—rious song of old."

Thank goodness it was clear. She had been so afraid there would be no snow, for three days after the contests at Laporte a thaw had set in, followed by two weeks of rain and sleet and more rain.

Thus Denis had been unable to visit the ruin, where she hoped to find the solution to her puzzle, either in the tower or in the mysterious chamber above the octagonal study. But the weather had not only spoiled all skiing, it had kept Jules Dulac at home. And she could not visit the ruin while he was there.

Fortunately she had had little time to think of anything but preparations for Christmas. There were presents to finish; puddings and cakes and candy to make; shopping to do. Denis had gone with Claire into Quebec for one day's shopping. They had lunched with Aunt Felice's sister and Claire had pointed out a tall, grey house, closely boarded up, in the next street. It belonged to their grandfather.

"When he is at home, Mamma stays part of the winter in town and entertains for him," Claire explained during lunch. "Last time I came, too. It is very gay in Quebec in winter."

"Especially when Tubby is here, *n'est-ce pas, ma chérie?*" said Aunt Suzanne.

But Claire declared primly that she had not seen Tubby for months and did not expect to see him.

The city was not at its best that day. A heavy fog hung over the river and there was a persistent drizzle that made it unpleasant to walk about the narrow, hilly streets. Yet the tall houses, with their steep roofs and gabled windows, the quaint old streets and the great *Château Frontenac* with its towers and turrets, made Quebec a storybook city, if a somewhat dismal one.

Not that the weather was any better in the country, or at least it had not been until two days ago when the temperature dropped suddenly, turning the rain to snow. And twelve hours later the country had a fresh white dress for Christmas. Clem had met Angelica's train with the sleigh when she came home from school and this morning they all had gone out on skis to cut the greens and select a tree. Tonight they would trim it.

> "The world in sol—emn stillness lay,
>   To hear the an—gels sing."

Denis glanced at the clock and went out to the kitchen for a peep at her pie, returned to play more Christmas music. She enjoyed the piano now that she did not have to practice hours each day in an effort to improve her technique. But the thought of how it would be at the end of the year of rest periodically troubled her. Since she was to be a pianist she could only hope the doctor was right when he said all she needed was a long vacation.

> "The dark night wakes, the glory breaks,
>   And Christmas comes once more."

Denis closed the hymnbook and stood up with a sigh of discomfort. Oddly enough the idea of being a pianist seemed less important than it had a year ago. Or was she just lazy? She hurried back to the kitchen and offered to knead the bread for Curly Rose as though to prove to herself that she wasn't.

When her pie was out of the oven Denis ran upstairs for paper and ribbon to tie up the lollipops she and Aunt Felice had made. Claire was busily wrapping presents in the next room and Angie had gone to the village with Uncle Guy. While she was looking for the ribbon, Denis heard sleigh bells and saw that they were back, Bruce Walker with them. Uncle Guy had let Angie and Bruce out before driving on to the barn.

Then Claire called her in to see the bathrobe that was her Christmas present for Curly Rose. The box was so large Denis helped tie it up and by the time she started downstairs Angie and Bruce had come in. They were standing in the hall below where Angie was tearing open a package that had come by mail.

"It must be mistletoe. It's from Carolina and that southern boy who visited the Cummings last summer promised to send me some. I'll tell Claire you are here in a minute, Bruce."

As she pulled off the wrappings and triumphantly lifted a large sprig of mistletoe out of its cotton, Angelica looked so pretty that Denis paused on the stairs to watch her. She had thrown off her fur coat but still wore the crimson hood that was so becoming. Deftly she tied the ribbon from her package on the sprig of mistletoe and handed it to Bruce.

"Will you put it up? There, over the doorway. You'll see a nail. You are so tall you can reach," Angie added, her tone and glance flattering him.

"It is the most beautiful piece we have ever had," she declared when the mistletoe was in place.

Her face was upturned admiringly and suddenly Bruce Walker had pulled her under the mistletoe and was kissing her.

It was not Denis's idea of a mistletoe kiss. She clutched the stair rail in dismay and stood frozen as a faint gasp told her she was not the only one who had witnessed it. Then Claire was gone but she could not seem to move. She watched Angie squirm free, raise one hand and claw it furiously across the man's face, then step back out of his reach, her black eyes flashing.

"I don't think I'll tell my sister you are here, Mister Bruce Walker. She is much too nice for you. Besides," Angie laughed suddenly, a light, malicious sound. "Besides, I don't think you'll be here much longer."

Had Aunt Felice been watching from the dining-room doorway all the time? Denis did not wait to find out. While the man made an awkward attempt to explain the incident as a joke, she turned and fled along the upper hall.

"Claire! Let me in. It's Dee. Oh, Claire, don't look like that," Denis said in distress when the older girl finally opened the door. "He isn't worth it."

"I know. When I saw his face as he snatched greedily at Angie——" Claire swallowed, turned away and pretended to look for a handkerchief before she finished. "You don't know how horrid it is to find someone you thought rather special —not like that at all. Ugh! And I was so easily taken in. *Quelle stupide!*"

"Not stupid," Denis objected. "Clem says you are too nice to be a judge of some people."

"Clem says," Claire repeated indignantly. "What has Clem to do with it?"

"Oh, nothing, of course. Except that he never liked Bruce," Denis said hastily. But suddenly she was convinced that Clem might have quite a lot to do with it. It was he who had met Angie's train yesterday, she remembered.

"I seem to have been well talked over," Claire said with dignity. "What did Clem say exactly?"

Denis hesitated, then decided to tell her. "He said you were too nice to handle a smoothie like Bruce Walker, that it took someone like Angie, who was a smoothie herself."

Denis chuckled at the remembrance of the scene in the

hall before she described the finish of it for Claire. "You should have heard Angie; it might have been Aunt Felice herself, in her grandest manner—'my sister is much too nice for you.'"

"But did he go? Because I simply cannot go down until——" Claire stopped as the doorknob was rattled impatiently.

"Claire! Are you there? Let me in."

And when the key was turned Angie skipped gaily into the room. "Claire! Guess who is downstairs? He is just back from Vancouver and Clem brought him out. Why you ever fought with such a honey! He's in the living room with Mamma and afraid to ask for you, just keeps looking toward the hall."

Angie paused to give her sister a quick survey before she urged, "Do go down and put him out of his misery, Claire. There's a huge white box under his coat and I haven't had a decent chocolate for months. Powder your nose and—run. I expect the box to be open when I get down."

As Claire finally started down the hall Denis said laughing, "Suppose it isn't candy?"

"It will be. Tubby always brings sweets, the super deluxe kind, too. If he had a two-carat engagement ring in his pocket he'd still have a box of chocolates under his arm. And that is my idea of a date." Satisfied that her sister was out of hearing, Angie added, "What's wrong with Claire?"

"We happened to be on the stairs when the mistletoe was hung," Denis explained simply.

"Oh! She saw?"

"Most of it."

"That insect!" said Angie scornfully. "I promised Clem I'd show him up but I didn't expect such a break—Claire watching and Mamma on hand to brush him out. What did Claire like about the creature anyway? The old—wolf!"

"You mean you and Clem planned——"

"We did not plan the scratched face. That was a Christmas present from me," Angie said gleefully.

"And I suppose bringing Tubby home was in the plan," said Denis.

"Why not? Come along, that candy must be open by now. And Tubby is a lamb. You'll like him."

Angelica's prediction was right. Denis did like Tubby. But whereas she had expected to find him plump and rather dull, he proved to be thin as a flag pole, almost as tall, and the exact opposite of what his nickname implied. He was witty and fun. He and Clem flung amusing insults at each other as they trimmed the tree after supper. Obviously he was deeply in love with Claire and the quarrel must have been patched up, for Claire never had looked prettier.

Midge, bemoaning the fact that Mr. Chip had not wakened for Christmas, was allowed to help for a time. But her aid consisted mainly in a curious inspection of each package in the heap waiting to be arranged under the tree.

"What could be in Dee's package from Grandpère?" she murmured as she examined the box.

"Hand me that angel with the broken wing, Midge," said Tubby who had been elected to trim the higher branches. "What is in the box from Paris? Why, a splosh evening gown."

Denis, secretly curious herself to know what was in the box, hastened to protest, "It couldn't be. How would Grandfather know my size? He has not seen me since I was seven or eight."

"But he knows what you look like," Midge assured her. "Because I wrote him a letter. All about you and how nice you were and I hoped he would come home for Christmas and bring me a myna bird."

"Margot!" Aunt Felice protested in alarm.

"I don't think we need worry about a myna bird yet," said Uncle Guy, smiling.

But Aunt Felice did not look entirely satisfied as she took Midge up to bed. A little later Clem left to answer the telephone and by the time he came back they had almost finished the tree. Denis was handing Tubby the last of the lollipops when Clem spoke.

"Dee! Want to do a good act for Christmas?" he asked bluntly, looking so grim Denis was taken aback.

She said in surprise, "Of—course. What is it?"

"It's Jeanpierre's grandmère. Broke her leg, compound fracture. Doctor can't give a general because her heart's bad."

Clem explained that the old Frenchwoman had asked for Jules. If he would play his fiddle while they set the bone, she could stand it. But unhappily old Jules was away.

"Jeanpierre wants to know if you'll come, Dee? Play and sing while they set it, eh?" Clem finished abruptly.

Denis, who could not bear to see anything hurt, who covered her ears if she heard an ambulance bell and closed her eyes when there was a screech of brakes that meant a possible accident, gazed at him appalled.

"Me!" she gasped.

"Yes, there's the piano Grandfather gave Dulac years ago when they thought Jeanpierre could learn to play. Probably it isn't in tune but you can manage."

"But—how can I——" Denis stammered. "My—music——"

"Is too important for a poor piano, not to mention an old peasant woman, I suppose," said Clem roughly. "All right, forget it. Have fun."

That was not what she had meant at all. Denis felt her eyes sting with the unfairness of it, even while she decided that Clem was the most hateful person she had ever known and she would never willingly speak to him again.

Aunt Felice said quietly, "It has been a long, busy day, this one. Denise is tired. I do not think it wise that she go——"

Angrily winking the moisture back, Denis interrupted. "Oh, but I must, Aunt Felice. I cannot see how my music will help, but I'll try."

As she walked to the piano, Clem flung a blunt suggestion after her. "Bring the Christmas hymns. And put on warm togs, it's nearly forty below. I'll be around with the sleigh in a jiffy."

There was no need to speak. Tubby and Uncle Guy tucked her into the fur rugs and they were off. It did not seem cold, the air was so dry and clear. Was that why the stars were brighter? As they skimmed along the road toward the hills, Denis gazed at the brightly spangled sky and forgot about Clem. It must have been a night like this, that first Christmas Eve long ago, when the Wise Men followed a star.

At the Dulac house, a kindly old priest was waiting with the doctor in the stuffy room that was kitchen and living room in one. Mère Dulac's wrinkled old face was white and dazed but she managed a weak "*bon soir*" as Denis took off her coat and hood and sat down at the piano.

It had been moved so that the patient could see as well as hear, and Denis could see her. Tempted to leave the hymns behind just because Clem had suggested them, she was now thankful she had not done so. The Frenchwoman could not understand the words but the message of hope in the Christmas music was universal. Only she must so play and sing that it would reach and help the old grandmère.

At first Denis had to summon all her courage to glance at the patient's face, see the spasms of pain and hear the faint moans when it was more than the old woman could bear. But gradually she found herself watching every change that she might know better what to sing and how.

"Si—lent night, ho—ly night,"

Denis watched the patient's face relax into a weary sort of peace at last. The doctor had finished his work and the grandmère had fallen into an exhausted sleep, but Denis sang softly to the end.

"Sleep in hea—ven—ly peace."

She did not need the doctor's tired smile of gratitude or the profuse thanks of the family whispered in French patois, to tell her that it was the most wonderful Christmas Eve she had ever known.

"Good job, Dee," said Clem briefly as he held her coat.

Then they were out in the cold air again and from the dis-

tant village came the faint sound of church bells. It was mid-
night. Denis sang happily as she climbed into the sleigh.

> "It came up—on the midnight clear
> That glo—rious song of old."

"Merry Christmas," said Clem, gathering up the reins.

Denis responded between yawns. Huddled into the fur nest,
she was suddenly aware of how tired she was, how desperately
sleepy. Because her head wanted to fall against Clem's shoulder
and she was determined it shouldn't, she tried to talk.

"The piano! The piano—was in tune—after—all."

When Clem did not answer, Denis tried to repeat it but she
was sinking beyond the ability to rouse herself, even when her
head fell over and the rug was tucked more firmly around her
shoulders and something brushed the end of her nose.

Even when Uncle Guy lifted her out of the sleigh at *Manoir
Laurent*, Denis only half woke up, smiling sleepily. She had
been dreaming that Nicolette kissed her under the mistletoe—
kissed her on the nose.

CHAPTER XVIII

"Je Me Souviens"

"I suppose this pattern would wear as well," Claire said judiciously. "Which one do you like, Dee?"

When Denis chose the one with the wide satin stripe which both had admired, Claire compared the pieces of damask again and finally ordered her linens in that pattern. Then the girls looked at blankets. Although the purchase of these must wait until Aunt Felice was with them, it was fun to look; it was fun having Claire engaged and helping choose her trousseau.

After seeing her cousin with Tubby Christmas Eve, Denis was not surprised by their sudden engagement. And to make it the more exciting, right after the first of the year Aunt Felice had brought Claire and herself to stay in Quebec. They were established for several weeks in the comfortable rooms of a Madame Robineau, a friend of the family who took a few paying guests, here not only for the purpose of ordering a trousseau but to attend the many parties given for the engaged couple. Angie was back at school and Midge was living at the convent during her mother's absence, but Uncle Guy usually joined them for the weekends and once in a while Clem came to town for one of the dances.

"You must wear the yellow dress tonight," said Claire on the way home. "This will be the best party of the winter and Tubby has someone very special for you. It is too bad Clem cannot come but Jean Chartier is a wonderful dancer and so—so *comme il faut*."

She had been speechless Christmas morning when she opened the box with the Paris label and lifted out the evening frock Tubby had predicted. It was more than "splosh." According to Angie it was dreamy, the perfect color for her cousin's golden-brown hair and brown eyes. How her grandfather had managed to choose a dress so suited to her, Denis would never cease to wonder. And since she felt at her best in it, perhaps the yellow frock would enable her to handle a French boy who was so—as he should be.

The girls turned into their own street presently, a short block whose last houses overlooked the square and the river. Claire ran impatiently up the steps and rang the bell but Denis paused to survey the corner house across the way, the one with an adjoining yard and stable behind a high board fence. This was the house, its lower floors tightly boarded up, that was her grandfather's Quebec home. Naturally she was curious about it, particularly after what she had seen the night before last when she awoke cold and listened for the whistler.

She had not heard him since the night they arrived. The room she shared with Claire overlooked the street and that first night Denis had tossed about long after her cousin fell asleep. When someone turned into the quiet street, whistling, she had slipped out of bed and over to the window where she could see a figure moving along the opposite sidewalk. The whistling ceased as the figure melted into the shadow of the fence and Denis crept thoughtfully back into bed to wonder about him until she fell asleep. Because he had been whistling the illusive melody of Hidden Pond, the song no one could name.

She never had heard him again. But the night before last she had wakened cold and finally, since she did not know where to find an extra blanket, had partially closed the window. That was how she happened to notice that the street light in front of her grandfather's house was out. And because of the unaccustomed blackness, high up on the top floor in one of the gable windows she could see, or thought she could, a chink of light.

Now, in the daylight, she stood looking thoughtfully at the closed house until Claire called impatiently, "Whatever are you gazing at, Dee? Marie says we are late for lunch and I cannot afford to miss a single bite."

Claire explained ruefully that she would need strength for

the duty call she and her mother must pay on Tubby's great-aunt that afternoon.

"She's just a curious old thing. Asks the most embarrassing questions. What will you do, Dee?"

Denis said there were lots of things she wanted to do. Actually she welcomed the opportunity to prowl about the historic old city by herself. Lines of snow trimmed the tall houses now and bells jingled cheerily as sleighloads of tourists were driven up and down the steep hills. But in spite of the tourists and the modern busses, Quebec managed to preserve its old-world air; the city remembered its stirring past. Denis thought its motto delightfully suitable—*Je Me Souviens*, I remember.

It was not only the citadel, high above the river, or the great stone St. Louis Gate, a reminder that Quebec was a fortified city, or all the things reminiscent of a more romantic time. At the Ursuline Convent nuns could still be glimpsed going quietly about their work and sometimes, as she walked through a side street, Denis could almost believe the old priest ahead was the famous Monseigneur Laval himself, that Count Frontenac still received visitors at Château St. Louis. Indeed, the fascination of the city increased as she knew it better so that she was always willing to see more of it. Today she would visit the old church of Notre Dame des Victoires and prowl about the lower town.

She did nothing of the kind. Because it happened that while she waited for her bus, two French lads came along and stood waiting for theirs. Had they been speaking English Denis would not have listened to their conversation. But they were jabbering in French and somehow it seemed perfectly all right to listen to a foreign language. Thus she soon discovered that they were on their way to a skating rink, eager to see a new skater. When they spoke of him as unknown but a boy who did beautiful spins, Denis gave up the idea of visiting Notre Dame des Victoires.

Instead, she climbed into the same bus with the French lads and left it when they did. At the rink she was early enough to get a seat near the ice and while she waited, Denis sat thinking about Jarret. Was he the unknown skater? She had not confided to anyone her suspicion that Jarret was training to be a professional. She had been willing to break her unspoken promise only when she thought him in danger.

Denis could understand Jarret's desire to prove his ability before facing his father; she was consious of a growing wish that she had a substitute as concrete to offer her mother. For how could she explain that the months at *Manoir Laurent* had taught her the happiness of working with people, that in spite of her love of music the isolated career for which she had been trained seemed less and less important or desirable?

Her reflections were interrupted by the appearance of the skaters and she leaned forward to inspect each one as they took a practice turn around the rink. Jarret was not among them. Unless—unless that slim, smallish boy in brown, who had come on too late for a practice round, was he.

The first number did not bring him near her, nor did the second. But then came the original-figure contest and Denis watched breathlessly as the boy moved with swift grace into a figure not only difficult but new to the audience. Not new to her, however. She had seen him do it at Laporte. There was enthusiastic applause as he completed his turn, and Denis leaned forward expectantly, since to avoid the next skater the boy must pass her seat. He was skating head down, as though the audience did not exist, and just before he reached her Denis spoke.

"Jarret!"

The low call brought his head up and the grey eyes looked straight into hers as they had that rainy day on the train. Then he had passed, picked up speed and was nearing the exit. As he left the ice, Denis jumped to her feet. Now that he had seen her he was unlikely to come back and she must speak to him.

She had trouble getting through the crowd, however, and difficulty in finding the skater's entrance. Misdirected by one of the guards, she reached it finally only to be told that the boy answering her description had left. At her crestfallen look, the doorkeeper stepped outside and peered up and down the street.

"*Voilà!* There he goes!"

With a hasty thanks Denis set off after the hurrying figure. She had covered less than a block when she knew Jarret had seen her and if he had not been held up by traffic she would have lost him, for it was almost dusk and a light snow was falling. He led her a circuitous route after that but Denis was too intent on the chase to notice where she was. When he rounded an unexpected corner she put on a burst of speed, slipped on an icy place concealed by the snow and arrived flat on her stomach. Thus it was from an awkward position that she peered down a comparatively empty street and found compensation for her tumble.

Jarret looked back, failed to see her because her head was practically on the sidewalk, and slowed down. Immediately Denis was up and after him, gaining appreciably before he reached the next turn, saw her and broke into a run. She skidded around the corner in pursuit only to bring up with a cry of dismay. Her quarry had escaped by leading her to a block so short he could sprint through it and disappear before she could see which way he turned. How exasperating of him!

Oddly enough there was something familiar about the block. Why it was her own, she realized and suddenly noticed something else. The snow had left a fresh carpet on which every footprint was visible and those of the boy ahead suddenly stopped. The snow was unmarked beyond a point opposite the fence that shut off her grandfather's stable yard.

But surely Jarret had not had time to climb the high board fence? Denis stared at it, baffled, until she saw the cross line that betrayed a door. She tried to push it open but either the door was fastened on the inside or someone was holding it. Could Jarret be living in the Laurent stable or the closed house? Was he the whistler then? As she recalled the chink of light in the gable window it seemed possible. But why was he so determined not to speak to her? She had not given him away and did not intend to. She merely wanted to ask him a question, a question curiously enough, about the song of Hidden Pond.

Slowly Denis crossed the street, pausing at the foot of her own steps to look thoughtfully back at the tall grey house with its adjoining stable yard. They suggested the customs of another day. Even her grandfather's house was part of the spirit of the city that remembered.

The spirit of—— With a startled exclamation Denis recalled where she had last heard the words, *L'esprit du pays*. Then, smiling to herself, she ran up the steps. And I, too, remember, thought Denis triumphantly. *Je me souviens*.

CHAPTER XIX

Locked In

DENIS slid out of her coat and tossed it on a chair before she looked thoughtfully out the window at her grandfather's closed house. It was the morning after the big dance and Clem, who had surprised them by coming to town for the party after all, had just taken her to breakfast before catching his train home. The invitation had been given jokingly, a kind of challenge—of course she would not be up in time.

But Denis was up, partly because a breakfast date sounded too novel to miss, but also because there was something she wanted to ask Clem. The breakfast, in the main dining room of the *Château Frontenac*, at one of the window tables from which she could see far down the St. Lawrence, had been an occasion she would long remember as part of the charm of Quebec. But when she asked if he could get the key to her grandfather's house for her, Clem shook his head.

"Grandfather did not leave a key with us."

This was disappointing. And it did seem strange, thought Denis, now that she was home and gazing resentfully at the board fence through which Jarret had disappeared. Was he hiding in the closed house? And if so, how did he get in? Unless—— She caught up her handbag and fished out of the zipper pocket two apparently unrelated scraps of paper—the ticket to Trois Lacs and a torn piece of grocery ad on the back of which was pencilled the melody of Hidden Pond. She stared at them, excited by the possibility of a connection between the two, a connection that might explain both. Then there was a knock on the door and Denis hastily thrust them back into the zipper pocket.

When it proved to be Madame Robineau, who wanted to

inspect the curtains and leave fresh bedspreads, Denis pointed impulsively across the street.

"Does Grandfather still use his stable?"

No, it was only a storehouse now, according to Madame.

Denis sighed. "I'd just love to see the inside of the house. Is it interesting?"

"But naturally. *Très intéressant*," Madame assured her.

"I do wish he had left a key," Denis said impatiently.

"So? He did leave a key. With me," the Frenchwoman said briefly. But the house would be black as night and cold like ice, not a wise place to visit.

Denis protested excitedly that she could wear a coat and take a flashlight.

"An adventure, eh?" said Madame Robineau. Yet perhaps she remembered the time when visiting a closed house would have meant that to her, for although she raised her eyebrows and looked faintly amused, she said abruptly that when she had inspected the curtains of the other rooms she would admit Denis to the house of her grandfather.

"You will say nothing to the others, no?" Madame Robineau cautioned.

Denis promised not to confide in a soul and was trying to act casual when Claire rushed in a few minutes later. Claire had been to a meeting of some kind and had just time to change before she met Tubby.

"What is that tune you are humming, Dee?" she demanded as she stripped off one dress and wriggled into another.

"You tell me. Jeanpierre sings it but claims he does not know the name."

"It sounds so familiar," said Claire. "And that reminds me. I promised the committee that you would play and sing for the Hospital Benefit, Dee. When he is here, Grandfather always plays for them."

"But Claire!" Denis exclaimed in startled protest, "I'm not—you—you didn't suggest me in his place?" she demanded horrified.

"Of course not. I just said you might be willing to do a few imitations at the piano. Tubby thinks they would pep up the program. And so does Mamma. Oh, there comes Tubby now and he hates to wait. Where are my gloves? You will do it, won't you, Dee?"

Then Claire was gone, leaving Denis completely taken aback. It was one thing to entertain Midge by imitating the way people sang. But to do that for a charity benefit! And for people who were accustomed to hear her grandfather play! What a crazy idea.

Not that it wouldn't be fun, she was thinking when Madame Robineau looked in to announce herself ready. And five minutes later, wrapped in a long cape, she led Denis across the street and unlocked the narrow door in the boarding, then the heavy front door inside.

"Should you take the cold, Madame Fraser will be angry. So do not remain long, eh?" the Frenchwoman warned before she went home, leaving the door in the boarding open.

When Denis closed the house door, however, the draft blew the outer door closed and she was suddenly in darkness, a still velvet blackness. Hastily she switched on her flashlight, parted the heavy draperies on her left and entered what must be the drawing room. It was a long, formal room, its furniture protected by ghostly dust covers. At the far end were more draperies and beyond them she found herself in a pleasanter room, with a piano, other musical instruments, a portrait of her grandfather above the fireplace, and big leather chairs.

But as she looked around Denis shivered. The house was so uncannily still. And was it the high ceilings that made her flashlight seem dim? She hurried a little as she walked back through the formal drawing room, stood at the foot of a long staircase and realized that her flash was giving less light every second, that the battery must be almost gone.

She could not explore the house without a flash, yet Denis was suddenly more relieved than disappointed. In the eerie stillness not only her inspiration of yesterday but the connection between Jarret's ticket receipt and a torn grocery ad seemed improbable. And suddenly her desire to explore the house was gone. But as she hastily opened the front door the fading light of her flash revealed an appalling fact. The door in the boarding had no knob, no catch, nothing she could grasp. It had locked itself and only a key, from the inside as well as the outside, would open it.

While Denis stood aghast, the flashlight went out and darkness engulfed her. She groped her way back to the staircase, sat down and told herself not to get into a silly panic. It was nothing but an empty house. And presently Madame Robineau would come over to find out why she was staying so long. A moment later she discovered that the house was not quite empty.

"O—oooh!"

Denis threw her flash wildly at whatever had scampered across her foot, dived through the unseen draperies, somehow felt her way to the end of the long room and through the second shroud of draperies. In one of the slippery leather chairs, with her feet gathered under her, she felt reasonably safe from a mouse. She had always thought the creatures appealing, especially in pictures. But here! In the dark! Would Madame Robineau never come back?

That Madame might return and, finding the door in the boarding closed, assume Denis had left the house, fortunately did not occur to her. She huddled in the leather chair and waited, waited for what seemed hours before she heard a sound. And then it was not the sound of a door opening or of Madame's voice. Was she dreaming? No, somewhere in the house, someone was playing the piano.

Mice forgotten, Denis scrambled up, felt her way back to the staircase, stubbing her foot on one chair and overturning another on the way. But as she mounted the long staircase, the music grew clearer. It came from the third floor, she discovered, pausing on the second flight at the sound of an all too familiar strain. Then, outside a door in the hall above, she stood for ten, fifteen, twenty minutes listening entranced

to some of the loveliest music she had ever heard. And the theme that ran through it was the elusive melody of Hidden Pond.

When the music stopped at last Denis was trembling with excitement. Cautiously she turned the knob, slowly pushed the door open and looked into a comfortable, sunlit room, whose unboarded windows overlooked the river. A fire blazed on the hearth, a coffee percolator gurgled on a small table and the floor about the piano was strewn with sheets of pencilled music. As the door squeaked a voice called out.

"It's finished, Jarret! I changed that last movement and my symphony is complete. Did you get the kipper? And fresh bread? I'm famished." Then the man at the piano swung about and saw Denis.

"*Bon Dieu!* Can it be my golden granddaughter? How in the name of all the saints did you get in here?" But the black eyes laughed a welcome as Denis came forward.

"The music!" she breathed. "You wrote it yourself. You were the old crony with the eye patch. That's why the Dulac piano was in tune. You borrowed it. And you had seen me before you ordered that dreamy frock. I suppose you ate the chicken, too," she accused. "And took that wild strawberry jam and——"

"I was hungry," Denis Laurent murmured.

"But the music cabinet? And Jarret's knife? And the ring? And"—Denis pointed at a gold pencil on the piano—"and that?"

Her grandfather chuckled. "Yes, that is the pencil your aunt accused the crow of filching. As for the cabinet, I needed some notes I had made in one of the books. I had a key to the house, you know. The ring? That was my little joke to keep you mystified."

But it was the ring that had given her a clue, Denis confessed. After seeing the old crony's hands she had studied the hand in the portrait and realized that they were very like. Only she could not understand how her grandfather could be the old crony if he was in England. Besides, Jarret's hand was also very like that in the portrait. Yet she could not believe Jarret had stolen the ring. Then, the significance of the ticket to Trois Lacs had struck her. If her grandfather, for some unfathomable reason, was the old crony and Jarret was staying with him, that would account for everything.

"You were here all the time then; here, or in the tower or the ruined *château*. But why? Why did you pretend to be in Africa and Australia?" Denis demanded.

The man at the piano studied her thoughtfully before he confided, "Because, my dear, for years I have wanted to write a symphony of my own, music that would interpret the spirit of French Canada, that would reflect its characteristic sounds.

"There is the warwhoop of Indians and there is the peaceful ringing of church bells, the leap of a fish in some woodland pool and the thunder of a breaking log jam; there is the swing of the river songs."

Denis put in enthusiastically, "And the crackle of ice. And sleigh bells. No wonder the theme melody was so familiar. It's beautiful music, Grandfather," she told him reverently.

The man smiled. "Thank you, my dear."

"But why did you hide in the ruin? And then here?"

"Because, my child, one cannot write a symphony and give concerts. One can practice in the morning, yes, give a concert in the afternoon perhaps and be social at night. But to create one must be alone."

Yet only on its soil, in its woods, among its people could he recreate the spirit of French Canada, Denis Laurent explained. So while he had letters mailed to them from abroad, he was working hard in the tower or the ruin, right under their noses.

"And until a curious granddaughter from the States came along," he added with a faint smile, "no one but Jarret suspected it."

"Jarret!" Denis exclaimed. "What about Jarret? He has been with you since he ran away, hasn't he? You approve? Of his being a skater?"

Her grandfather shrugged. "In a sense, yes. It was the ambition of a boy who wanted only to escape the mine. When he came to me I made a bargain with Jarret. If he would give a few hours each day to the serious study of music then he could stay with me and practice his skating. I told him it was a compromise to salve my conscience, but actually it was because I knew Jarret to be the real musician of the family, the one with talent. And now I think he has given up the idea of being a professional skater, eh, Jarret?"

"It was a kid's notion," agreed the boy in the doorway.

He scowled at Denis over his armful of bundles. "How did you get in here?" he demanded.

"Madame Robineau let me in. Why wouldn't you speak to me the other day? After all, I knew about the skating and had not told anyone."

"I couldn't let you find Grandfather before he finished his symphony, Miss Nosey," said Jarret.

"Well, it is finished now," Denis Laurent announced. "So run down for an extra plate and cup, Jarret. We'll celebrate by inviting Denis to *déjeuner*."

When Jarret had gone, Denis looked anxiously at her grandfather.

"You said Jarret was the only real musician in the family. What—about me?"

Denis Laurent cleared his throat, hesitated, said at last, "Tell me. Why do you want to be a pianist?"

"Because——" Denis stopped. "I don't. I'd rather be someone's cook," she confessed, suddenly aware that it was true.

"Ah! And do you know why? Do you know why you broke down under so much practice? Because you lack the talent to be a great pianist."

"But I have to earn my living. And—and mother expects it. What else can I do?"

The man shrugged. "You might teach. You would probably be a good accompanist. You may have some of your father's ability to act. Don't ask me; ask yourself.

"You see," he continued, "we each have a hidden pond of talent, however shallow it may be. The point is to find it."

There were some unfortunate people who never had an opportunity to seek their pond but were forced to jump into the nearest lake and swim unhappily about without ever getting anywhere. Others chose the wrong pond and foundered. It was because his father could not see that the asbestos mine was not Jarret's pond, never could be, that he, Denis Laurent, had been willing to conspire with the boy.

"And the farm is Clem's pond, I suppose," Denis said ruefully. "But what is mine?"

"That, my child, is something you must find out for yourself. But forget you were going to be a concert pianist. Think about making music for those who need it. I am not sure, you know, that it isn't the more important thing," he added thoughtfully.

CHAPTER XX

The Bride's Bouquet

"WHY CAN'T PEOPLE get married without all this fuss?" Clem demanded.

It was warm on the back gallery, where Angelica was painting cards for the refreshment tables and Clem, already dressed for the occasion, lolled in a deck chair watching her and complaining. Why all the fuss? Here he was, the only calm person in the house, the only one ready.

Since it was two hours before the first guest could be expected, he sounded altogether too complacent and Angie hastened to puncture his self-satisfaction.

"Suppose you have to move the piano at the last minute? Or climb the ladder again?"

"You would think of that," Clem grumbled. "But why all this ado? Everyone in a dither! Even Ma Tante is jittery and Tubby's as jumpy as a fish. He ought to be snoozing here in the sun like his best—man."

Clem's voice trailed off lazily. As his eyes closed, Denis slid through the screen door and offered Angelica a sample of bride's cake without making a sound. Angie rubbed her stomach in a pantomime of noiseless approval, whereupon the cake-maker dropped down on the gallery step and began to nibble the piece she had intended for Clem. She could not start to dress yet because her mother, tired after the long journey, was resting in her room. Besides, there were still things to be done.

But Denis was glad to idle for a few minutes. The air was fragrant with all the scents of spring, the fields were freshly green and the apple orchard was a frothy pink drift between the house and the brook. What a perfect day for the wedding! In the living room she could hear her grandfather at the piano, softly playing over the wedding music.

Angie used her last card to print a sign "Just Married" and was about to clean the brush when there was a distinct snore from Clem. The girls exchanged an amused glance. Then Angelica flashed Denis a mischievous look and again dipped the brush in green paint. With infinite caution, so that only once did he even stir, she stroked it over Clem's eyebrows.

Had Clem been wearing his old clothes, or if his hair had been anything but red, he might not have looked to ridiculous with bright green eyebrows. As it was, Denis had to bury her head to smother her laughter. Until the sound of Midge's voice reminded her that she had promised to press the ribbon for the flower girl's basket of rose petals. Still choking with mirth, she hurried back into the house, leaving Angie to tell the best man he was not quite as ready as he had thought. She did not think of him again until she was getting dressed herself, because there had been a little trouble with Midge.

"No! You may do nothing of the kind, Margot," Aunt Felice said firmly.

"But, Mamma! He has never seen a wedding. And Nicolette will be there; Charcoal, too. And Muff will probably sneak in. Why can't Mr. Chip go? He will stay on my shoulder."

"Oh, Margot! You are old enough to know why," her mother said impatiently. "A wedding is a solemn occasion. The flower girl with a chipmunk on her shoulder would make it more like a circus. You wanted your hair cut for the wedding, is it not so, *ma petite?* Then you must not behave like a madcap in braids."

"But Mamma——"

"I have said no, Margot. Do not speak of it again."

Aunt Felice hurried off and Denis undertook to console Midge, pointing out that Nicolette would sit quietly beside her master under the piano and Charcoal would stay with Nicolette. But suppose Muff did get in and Mr. Chip saw her.

Suppose he got flustered and panicky in the middle of the ceremony?

"You wouldn't want to spoil Claire's wedding, would you?" said Denis.

"Of course not. But Mr. Chip would stay on my shoulder. Truly he would, Dee."

"Maybe he would, and thus steal the show. A wedding is the bride's day, Midge. You wouldn't want people to look at Mr. Chip instead of Claire?"

No, Midge did not want that. She went thoughtfully off,

Uncle Guy
Aunt Felice
and Midge

without further argument, presumably to explain to Mr. Chip why he could not attend the wedding.

With Midge on her mind, Denis had completely forgotten the best man and his green eyebrows until, as she started to dress, she heard him call to someone.

"I'll have to go after the ice cream. The man just phoned to say his car has broken down and Jeanpierre has gone home to dress. But tell Tubby not to worry. I'll be back in plenty of time. And I'm all set."

Clem did not get back in plenty of time however. The bride was in the upstairs hall with her attendants, ready for the signal to start down, when Mrs. Fraser came up and explained that they were waiting for the best man.

Claire was disturbed. "Oh, dear! Tubby will be in a state."

"Not if he is chatting with that jolly Father Insley, as he probably is," Denis told her.

"I think I hear the car," said Midge who was peering out the window overlooking the back gallery. The short hair was flattering to her piquant little face and in her flower girl's dress she was a picture.

"Oh, Midge, don't press so close to the screen," Sally Clarkson warned. "A flower girl with a black nose would be a fine sight."

There was a smothered exclamation from Angelica. But no one heard because it was Clem's car. And now someone was running along the gallery below and Denis could hear Uncle Guy's voice.

"Go in through the end window, Clem. Tubby and Dr. Insley are waiting behind the screen. I say! Just a minute."

The girls formed a line, ready to start down. Midge, with her basket of rose petals, was first, followed by Sally and Denis. Then came Angelica as maid of honor, and last of all, the bride. Sally turned to whisper something to Angie and Denis reminded Midge not to hurry.

"Scatter the rose leaves slowly, as though you were showering—— Midge!" Denis gasped, her appalled gaze on the *moving* rose petals. The child's hand hastily pressed them down but not before Denis had seen the head of a curious chipmunk.

It was too late to do anything because Uncle Guy, waiting at the foot of the staircase, gave the signal to start down. No one else had seen Mr. Chip. But would they? Would Midge be able to keep him hidden in the rose petals? Denis thought, as she passed, that the bride's father wore a peculiar expression, not worried or sad, but as though he wanted to laugh. Perhaps it was only her guilty knowledge that at any moment a chipmunk might escape and turn the wedding into a circus.

In spite of her anxiety she realized that her grandfather was playing the wedding march beautifully as she and Sally walked a few steps behind Midge down the long room. Before the fireplace, which had been banked with greens and apple blossoms, stood Father Insley facing the groom and his best man. Could he, too, have seen the chipmunk? It seemed to Denis that his jolly, round face was curiously red as he began to read the solemn words of the familiar service.

"I will," said the groom, his voice low but confident. And Claire's response was clear and sweet.

It was when the best man handed Tubby the ring that something suddenly went wrong with the bride. Could she be crying? There was a stir of apprehension among the silent guests, followed by a tense stillness as the ceremony was concluded and the blessing given.

Scarcely was it over before Denis leaned down and whispered to Midge, "Slip out the window and take him up to his box," she warned. "Quickly! Before they miss you."

When she straightened, the best man was kissing the bride who was giggling hysterically and Denis exchanged one horrified look with Angelica before she joined in the laughter that swept the room.

Clem, tall and red-headed, wearing the self-satisfied air of having performed his part of the ceremony in good order, was still completely unconscious of the fact that his eyebrows were bright green.

Until Sally warned Midge about getting a black nose from the screen, Angie had not thought about Clem, had forgotten her failure to tell him he was not quite ready. Besides, he would have discovered the damage for himself. How could she know that Clem would have to dash off for ice cream? that no one would see him until his return when he had raced straight for the end window without hearing his father's second call?

The bride and groom were too happy to be resentful. But Aunt Felice was so indignant when Angelica was obliged to confess it was her doing, that Clem turned from the mirror to which someone had led him and spoke in her defense.

"Don't be too hard on her, Ma Tante. I was being pretty smug about the calm poise of a best man. Serves me right."

And certainly the green eyebrows, which he refused to touch, added gaiety to the occasion. Perhaps they even inspired the bride to mischief, Claire who was normally so sensible. It was after the wedding supper, when she had started upstairs to change and had turned, ready to toss her bouquet.

In the hall below, Angie and Denis and Sally, with two or three other girls, stood with upstretched arms as Claire laughed down at them and chanted the old rhyme.

"Look ye, pretty maidens, standing in a row,
Whoever catches this, the next bouquet shall——"

And then, over the heads of the girls, straight into the surprised and reluctant hands of the best man, went the bride's bouquet. Clem was a study in red and green as he held it awkwardly, muttered something about turpentine, and vanished.

It was after Tubby and Claire had driven off, when she was looking for Midge, that Denis saw him down under the apple tree at the corner of the orchard. Could it be possible Clem was angry at being made the clown of the wedding? He looked so solemn as he leaned on the fence gazing across the fields. Denis walked across the field in that direction, because he might know what had become of Midge and anyway she wanted to tell him that her mother had just agreed she could go to South America next winter with her grandfather.

He and Mrs. Fraser had had a long conversation alone the previous evening after which her mother had seemed resigned to the fact that Denis would never be a concert pianist. She was willing moreover that she should stay on at *Manoir Laurent* since her own work kept her not only busy but often away from home. She seemed to like the place and had promised to return for a real visit late in the summer when her work was less demanding.

"Good enough," Clem said gruffly when Denis had told him the news. But he did not look around.

Denis leaned over the fence herself. "We'll miss Claire, won't we?" she said tentatively. "But it was a beautiful wedding, wasn't it?"

"Think so?" Clem shrugged, then confided abruptly, "See that stretch of land the other side of the brook? It takes in some woodland and Birch Lake as well as that piece. Grandfather calls it *Petite Laurent*. He just offered it to me."

"But how wonderful!" said Denis.

"I turned it down."

"Why, I thought that was what you wanted most, a farm of your own."

"I did. But I've changed my mind. A farmer ought to have a wife."

Denis laughed. "That should be easy. You caught the bride's bouquet, didn't you?"

But Clem only scowled. "I'm not having any, thanks."

"Well you don't need to be so disagreeable about it. Have you any idea how homely you look, Clem Fraser, with your chin thrust out in that belligerent fashion? Imagine turning on marriage, after such a beautiful wedding, just because Angie——"

"Really, Dee," Clem flared, "for a girl who has a wonderful career ahead of her—and even Grandfather said you had after he heard you do those musical imitations at the Hospital Benefit—you're pretty stupid sometimes."

Denis opened her mouth indignantly, hesitated and then murmured sweetly, "Am I?" Then, after a moment she added, "But not so stupid I don't know when I've been kissed on the nose."

She held her breath after she had said it, wishing she hadn't as she watched the hand on the fence beside hers. Perhaps, after all, she had dreamed that kiss on Christmas Eve. And then, just as Clem's hand released its fierce grip on the rail and covered her own, there was a discreet cough behind them.

"Have you seen anything of that poodle of mine?" said Denis Laurent when they turned in guilty haste.

"Nicolette? Why—why I think I saw her chase a rabbit down through the orchard," said Clem.

"Thanks. I'll have a look."

He started on but Denis checked him, "Oh, Grandfather! I think Clem has changed his mind about *Petite Laurent*. Or anyway, he is—going to."

"Good! I rather thought he might." The black eyes twinkled. "Or that someone might change it for him."

Denis Laurent went on and his granddaughter leaned over the fence again, content that he knew, as she did, that she had found her hidden pond.

Clem frowned down at her before he said grimly, as though the words were dragged from him, "It is stupid, Dee, to give up your music, the sort of career you might have, to—to be a farmer's wife."

"Don't you think it depends on the farmer? Of course if he won't let me sing and does not think music important and always insists on kissing me on the end of the nose and——"

She stopped because it was not possible to go on when Clem was holding her so close and kissing her properly. But when they leaned over the fence again, Denis picked up where she had left off.

"And who said anything about giving up music? I can still

play and sing for people who need it and Grandfather says that is the important thing. Now—shall we decide where you are going to build our house while I am in South America?"

The End

www.ingramcontent.com/pod-product-compliance
Lightning Source LLC
Chambersburg PA
CBHW020634180626
46816CB00003B/964